BEYOND THE FRONTIERS

DEUCES WILD BOOK ONE

ELL LEIGH CLARKE

MICHAEL ANDERLE

LMBPN

DISRUPTIVE IMAGINATION

BEYOND THE FRONTIERS TEAM

Thanks to the JIT Readers

Kim Boyer
James Caplan
Mary Morris
Kelly O'Donnell
Daniel Weigert
Larry Omans
Joshua Ahles
Peter Manis
John Ashmore
Paul Westman
Micky Cocker
Thomas Ogden

If I've missed anyone, please let me know!

Editor
Lynne Stiegler

PROLOGUE

The name is Nickie. Meredith Nicole Grimes. I don't know if the Meredith bit was after the Empress' mom or the moon rock they settled on, but either way, my friends call me Nickie.

My childhood was pretty normal—if you call growing up amongst the Empress' inner circle normal. Granddad is one of her Bitches...which meant I had privileges and, well, expectations laid upon me. I didn't ask for any of it, the enhancements or the special treatment.

Don't get me wrong. It was fun, and I grew up loved and cared for. Everyone was like family. As kids we called the people Mom and Dad served with "Aunt" and "Uncle."

One of my "uncles" was the all-powerful commander of everything in the Empire. And even more so when the former Empress left, with the Federation.

My favorite aunt was named Tabitha. She would spend hours with me, teaching me how to shoot, and how to tear down the weaker sex, otherwise known as males. And secretly, how to drink. She was the best.

But Aunt Tabitha left to serve her Empress. Granddad John Grimes, too. I hate him. It's his fault Aunt Tabitha went away. There isn't a day that goes by that I don't feel the pain of her loss.

Even though she's not dead.

She may as well be.

After she left things got pretty rough. I was pretty much told to shape up or ship out.

So I shipped out.

Five years, I was told. After that, I needed to come back and carry on the family business: ruling the Federation, and enforcing the will of the former Empress.

I've spent the last few years of my exile swallowing liquor and drugs to try not to feel, but you know how that goes. You end up in seedy places, and before you know it you're in the middle of a gunfight and your enhancements kick in to keep you alive.

Well, if you're one of the former Empress' chosen, that is.

My enhancements had been deactivated when I stopped living that life, and I was glad of it. Enhanced metabolism would flush shit out of my bloodstream too quickly.

And life was good. It was fine. I'd spend my days drinking and gambling and...avoiding. So there I was, about to have my brains splattered across the wall, when everything kicked in, including my natural impulse for self-preservation. Long story short, I ended up taking out the lowlifes who started the trouble, rescued a damsel or two on the way, and then stole the ship with the other hundred or so Skaines on board.

Thankfully, Meredith, my personal onboard (and until that time, dormant) EI, had it covered. She locked the doors to keep them in there and me out here, then got us underway.

Oh yeah, and then there's Grim, or Grim'zee P. Bonesticker. No relation, but it turns out that we have history. Or at least our grandparents did. Anyhow, he seemed kind of decent, and since I would need a chef at some point anyway, it was the beginning of a beautiful friendship.

Now I'm here on this godforsaken ship with about a hundred Skaines locked in various rooms over the ship... all waiting like caged animals for their time to strike.

This is my story.

CHAPTER 1 NICKIE

Rebus Quadrant, Aboard the *Penitent Granddaughter*

The ship wasn't bad, all things considered. An engine. Guns. A bridge. A galley. A lot of space and other assorted rooms.

It had all the bits and bobs that make up a ship.

Nickie paused mid-step when the door to her left was thumped on loudly, as if a rhinoceros were trying to charge through it. She scowled at it menacingly, can in one hand, the fork in the other raised halfway to her mouth.

She kicked the door and kept walking as a barrage of guttural Skaine profanity followed her down the corridor. It rang out from behind various doors as she walked past them, just to drive the point home.

Whatever the point was.

Some elaborate version of "fuck off," more than likely.

The ship would have been better without all the excess *baggage*. There were too many people she didn't want on board, even if they were locked behind their doors like vicious little fuckhead gerbils in their cages.

With a sulk in her step, she made it to the bridge.

Grim spared her a glance over his shoulder for just a second before turning his attention back to the console in front of him. With just him on the bridge and Meredith keeping quiet for the moment, the space was as silent as a crypt.

Nickie wrinkled her nose at the comparison and shook her head to clear the mental image. No one needed to be thinking about something like that, even if it wasn't entirely inaccurate—considering how she had acquired the ship.

"The job listings in the database are...intriguing." Grim settled on the carefully neutral word as Nickie flopped down in the captain's chair. She sat sideways, leaning against one armrest with her legs thrown over the other.

"Slave trafficking, weapons dealing, drug- and people-smuggling," he listed, scrolling through the text on the console. His tone warred between discomfort and disgust. "Five hundred Yollins in this one exchange alone," he noted. Disgust won. "Considering this is all every shade of horrible, why doesn't the Federation do anything about it?"

He glanced up from the console at her again.

Nickie shrugged her free shoulder. "They probably don't even know it's all happening."

She shoved another bite into her mouth. Speaking with her mouth full, she added, "It's not like they broadcast it to everyone who wants to listen that they are doing all that." She flapped a hand at the console as she said it. "Back channels and black markets, and all that stuff."

She shoved another bite into her mouth.

Grim's eyes narrowed slightly. "I could make you actual food, you know," he pointed out for the fifth time in the last few hours. "Something with actual nutrients. And taste."

Nickie clicked her tongue at him. "No time for all that." Her words were muffled as she shoved another bite into her mouth, possibly just to spite him and his distaste. "We need to figure out what to do next, after all. Meredith!"

She straightened up slightly and swallowed too soon, so she had to pound a fist against her chest for a second. "Any update on where we might be able to drop off all this extra cargo?" she asked once she was sure she wasn't actually going to choke. "They're sort of loud and rude, you know? I feel very unwelcome."

"Yes," the EI answered simply, voice spilling out of the bridge speakers. "If I could make a suggestion, we'll be passing right by the Minerva Trading Outpost, and we should restock while we have the chance."

"Okay..." Nickie replied slowly, less agreeing and more acknowledging. "But we'd have to dock to do that, and we have all..." She trailed off, and settled for waving one arm toward the door she had just walked through a few moments before, encompassing all of the Skaines locked up all throughout the ship. "I don't think that would go swimmingly. Just a hunch."

"You *did* steal their ship," Grim pointed out reasonably. "And you *are* holding them hostage."

Nickie rolled her eyes. "Judge-y, much?" She scoffed, one hand settling awkwardly on her hip. "You didn't have a moral compass while I was saving your ass."

Grim shrugged, disinclined to rise to the bait. "All I'm saying is that *we* could be seen as the bad guys here—at least on a technicality."

Nickie snorted and slumped down farther in her seat. "Never pay attention to technicalities," she advised, though she sounded slightly sullen as she said it. "Unless they're in your favor. Anyway, loads of sci-fi heroes from the archives worked out of stolen ships. I'm following a precedent."

"How noble," Grim deadpanned. "Name one of these heroes."

"Doctor Who?" Nickie suggested, twisting her wrist so the handle of the fork clattered in a circle around the edge of the can.

"Any others?" Grim asked pointedly, cocking his head to one side.

There was a pause before Nickie suggested haltingly, "Han Solo?"

"Didn't he win his in a card game?" Grim asked, sounding distinctly unimpressed.

"Ah, right!" Nickie snapped her fingers. "Cards. Remind me to pick up a deck once we're docked."

Grim opened his mouth to reply, but Meredith cut him off.

"Perhaps if you feed them they'll quiet down," she suggested evenly. "It's been roughly twelve hours, after all."

Nickie blinked at one of the speakers. "But he's a—oh." She cut herself off. "You mean the Skaines. I guess that's worth a shot." She supposed it *had* been enough time for anyone to get hungry, and she was pretty sure she hadn't locked any of them in the galley.

"I can help with that," Grim volunteered, even if he already sounded slightly long-suffering about it. Or possibly about the sudden change of topic. It was hard to tell. "I'll probably need more supplies, though."

Nickie hummed a long, sustained note as she mulled that over, dropping the mostly empty can to the floor as she did. She crossed one leg over the other on the armrest, bobbing one foot casually in the air as she pondered their options.

"How about this," she suggested slowly, folding her arms over her middle. When the gesture made her slide even farther down on her seat, she steadfastly pretended that she had meant for that to happen—even when she had to squirm gracelessly back into a partially-upright position. "Once we get to the Minerva Outpost, you go off and get whatever supplies you'll need to keep the kitchen stocked and everything fed to whatever standard you plan on. I don't know how all that works anyway."

"Clearly," Grim drawled in reply, glancing down at the can. Nickie shushed him sharply.

"While you're doing that," she continued as if he hadn't said anything, "I'll get whatever ship's supplies we'll need. Sound like a plan?" she asked, finally swinging her legs to the floor so she would stop sliding all over the place. She accidentally kicked the can aside as she did.

"I have no complaints," Grim agreed, and he pushed himself away from the console and started heading toward the door.

"Where are you going?" Nickie called after him, baffled, turning to peer after him around the back of the chair.

"To take stock of the kitchen," he answered. "If I'm

restocking it, I would like to know what's already in there," he reasoned, as the door opened to let him pass.

"You have fun with that," Nickie called sarcastically, just before the door slid closed behind him. She slid down low in her seat.

If she *had* locked anyone in the galley, she supposed Grim would find out as soon as he got there. It would probably be funny. But she was supposed to at least be something like responsible in that moment, and she sighed slowly. Ships didn't take care of themselves, after all, much to her disappointment.

Meredith? Give me the update. What should I worry about getting once we're at the outpost?

She didn't bother speaking out loud, since there was no one else on the bridge to keep in the loop.

Immediately, text began appearing on the HUD, a list compiling itself in the corner of Nickie's vision.

I've had some thoughts on that already, Meredith replied. *I've been sorting through the ship's systems. The maintenance and the upkeep have been slacked on.*

Just regular slacking? Nickie wondered suspiciously. *Or are you just trying to sound diplomatic?*

It's nothing you won't be able to take care of with relative ease, Meredith assured her.

Nickie couldn't decide if that actually qualified as an answer to her question, but she didn't bother to ask. She could recognize when Meredith was just trying to be a troll.

A few hours passed and Nickie sighed loudly, clearly bored with all the waiting around and travel. This was a far cry from her old life of getting up, drinking, brawling, gambling, and then collapsing in an unconscious heap again.

Who knew that real life could be so...mundane?

Says the girl with a shipful of Skaines waiting to tear her apart at the first opportunity.

All right, Meredith. God! Do I ever just get some time to think my own thoughts?

Not now that I've been activated, I'm afraid.

Shit.

Nickie's mind compulsively flicked to all the dirty thoughts she'd had over the years, that she would rather no one be privy to. She was going to have to keep an eye on that, or figure out some kind of firewall that would fence in her "adult content" thoughts.

While you're figuring out how to do that, I thought you might like to know that I've found some information in your system. It has some important content that you might like to know.

What? I need a systems upgrade? My drug-induced lifestyle has taken its toll on my nanocytes.

No. Well, not exactly. Although we're going to have to visit a Pod-doc for a tune-up at some point.

Well? What is it?

It's your aunt.

My aunt is in my system?

No.

Nickie immediately started feeling emotional.

Well, what about her? she urged, trying not to let the feelings take over her body.

It seems she uploaded something on your system for me to discover once you rejoined the fold.

I haven't exactly *rejoined the fold,* Nickie corrected, still distracted by the news she was dreading hearing.

But you've activated me, which means something. In any case, I thought you should know about it.

What is it, then?

A file.

Of what?

I don't know. Would you like me to open it?

Yes.

Are you sure? We don't know what it could be.

Yes. Open it. It's from Aunt Tabitha, so I want to know.

Meredith was quiet for a moment. *Turns out it's a series of diary entries, with time-delay locks on it segment by segment.*

Why the time delays?

Maybe she wants you to take your time with it?

Nickie's mind spiraled, wondering about the possibilities.

Maybe she wants me to "get" each piece and not jump ahead. Maybe it's a count down?

She shook her head in disbelief. Pulling her feet down off the console, she sat up in the Skaine-sized pilot's chair.

Send it to my viewing device. I'd like to read it. That is...

Her voice trailed off and she stared into space, preoccupied by her thoughts and feelings. *Is there any part that is unlocked?*

There is. Sending the cover letter now.

Nickie sat in the dimly-lit bridge of the stolen ship, her eyes flicking from left to right, reading the words that were superimposed on her vision.

Dearest Nickie -

I know you were upset when I left. I'm so sorry. I miss you terribly. Every day.

I wanted to explain to you, and for you to understand. But I know now that you were too young. So I figured I'd wait...and try to explain it to you again when you were older.

I hacked your EI and left you a series of messages. Well, diary entries, really. My goal was to be there for you, even though I couldn't be there in person. I hope that through you reading these entries I can perhaps save you some of the pain I've been through. Maybe shortcut some of the lessons you'll have to learn. And hopefully allow you to know that I am with you still, and that you are loved.

I know that when I went through some things, I wished I had someone to guide me. I feel bad for not being there to guide you and help you avoid the pain and suffering I've been through as I've grown in what I hope is wisdom. I hope that by reading about my adventures and heartbreaks you'll come to realize that you're not alone, and that you too will get through everything you'll have to face with the courage and spirit that I know you have.

And one day, I hope that you can understand that I had to do my duty. Our Empress needed me, and my place was with her. But just know, there isn't a day goes by that I don't think of you, and miss you terribly.

Until we meet again, all my love, always,

Aunt Tabitha

Nickie swiped a tear from her face. She sniffed, her

eyes darting to the bridge door to make sure no one else was going to see her in this state.

Would you like me to upload the first entry to your device for reading?

Yes. Yes I would. Thank you, Meredith.

Nickie got up from her seat. *In fact,* she continued, *if Grim comes looking for me, can you let him know I'm resting in my quarters.*

Very good. I'll tell him. You have forty minutes until we reach the trading post.

Thanks.

Nickie swiped at her face again and strode off the bridge to the corridor beyond.

Rebus Quadrant, Approaching Minerva Trading Outpost, Aboard the *Penitent Granddaughter*, Nickie's Quarters

Safely ensconced in her still-new and novel quarters, Nickie flopped onto the bed. It was firm, and a tad smaller than she would have liked. The damn Skaines weren't the tallest beasts in the land.

With a mere thought, her systems adjusted her reading device—which was part of a nifty HUD package she'd had installed in her eyes years ago somewhere in the galaxy during—over her retinas. It had been a long time since she had read anything of length this way. It felt almost as if she were embarking on a new habit. A reading habit. Normally the only reading she did was Keep Out signs, or quick translations in bars or on dating sites.

Oh yeah, and the odd poker course, so she could slay

her drunken opponents with skill and finesse. But those weren't long form.

Now, faced with this new mysterious file from her aunt and seeing that there was lots of text, she settled in for a new experience.

Intrigued and on tenterhooks at what her aunt had in store for her, she shuffled the file back to the start, directing the interface with her conscious intentions, and began to read.

CHAPTER 2 TABITHA

Yoll Quadrant, QBSS _Meredith Reynolds_, Never Submit-Never Surrender Bar

Angie looked down into her drink and tried to focus on anything except the pain in her heart. She ached with it, day in and day out.

Manny had been everything to her. There was no joke she heard that she didn't want to tell him. There was no day she didn't want to go home and see him in their small set of rooms. There was no dinner she didn't want to eat with him.

And he'd always been the better cook, too, so dinner was shit twice over now. She couldn't stand in the kitchen with a beer and smell the hot peppers and spices he was cooking with as he joked with her about their days, and when she ate, she ate alone at their tiny table in an apartment that was the size of a small box, but still felt too big without him here.

She had never realized that when your heart broke, it actually felt like *physical* pain.

"You doing all right, honey?" The bartender, Lilah, came by to slide another full glass across the bar to Angie.

"Yeah. Yeah, I'm all right." Angie managed a smile.

Lilah watched her carefully. Her warm brown eyes and easy manner hid a keen sense of observation. She had seen enough heartbroken people come into this bar that she recognized the look.

In her experience, there were three stages of heart-break: shock, wallowing, and recovery.

Angie was wallowing. Lilah didn't use the term cruelly. Everyone needed to wallow sometimes. After the shock passed, there was no way to get through all the grief without allowing yourself to feel it.

As a bartender, she spent the most time with the wallowers. People in shock were still trying to pretend everything was fine. People who were recovering still came in, but they shared a beer with their friends or their memories—happily—so she could spend her time on the new wallowers.

Lilah cleared away the two empty glasses from in front of Angie and busied herself with cleaning them. She could use the automated dishwasher in the back, but she was guessing that Angie would want to talk.

She was right. Angie watched as Lilah made quick work of the two glasses, leaving them spotless and back on the shelf.

Her voice beckoned Lilah when she admitted, "I miss him so much. It's been months, and I still think about him every day."

Lilah looked up. Angie had already taken a huge swallow of the third beer, and she guessed that Angie was trying to get drunk so she would forget about her man.

It wouldn't work, but that was something every drunk person had to find out for themselves.

"What happened?" Lilah kept her tone light but her face serious. She had learned that no matter how big or small an issue was, it was all-encompassing for the person who came into her bar to escape it.

Angie paused for a moment before she answered, then opened her mouth to speak, lost her composure, and took another drink of her beer instead. Tears trembled in her eyes as she said the words, "He died on the *Recalcitrant*."

She had never said that out loud before. In the wake of the tragedy, everyone who needed to know already knew. She had been contacted by the relevant people in Manny's chain of command and supported through the funeral by the other people who grieved for him.

Everyone on the *Carda*, her ship, also knew.

But after a while, everyone else seemed to get past it. Angie, however, was still trying to wrap her head around the fact that Manny was never coming back. Every time she realized it anew it hit her in the chest all over again. She wanted to scream each time

It just hurt so damned much.

She kept trying to force herself to acknowledge it, but it never seemed to get *better*.

So she was here.

Lilah's heart twisted for the poor woman. She had seen enough grieving people to note the strength in Angie's tone, and what was left of her determination. Angie would get through this. But Lilah had also seen enough grieving people to know that Angie couldn't realize that yet, not the first time. Hopefully, there wouldn't be a second time.

"Death is what happens in war," Lilah wiped the bar in front of her.

Angie nodded. "I know. I *do* know."

"Never thought you didn't, honey. Just helpful to hear it out loud sometimes." Lilah didn't give any opinions on any of it. That wasn't her role right now. "Tell me about him."

Angie looked up, appreciation in her eyes. She knew her friends didn't want to hear stories about him anymore. They thought she was not moving on properly. "His name was Manny. He had the most amazing smile, and it lit up the whole room. His mother was Colombian, and he would sing these old songs... He teased me in Spanish, too. I never knew what he was saying. He was an amazing cook. He swept me off my feet, he was so gentlemanly." She looked down at her beer.

"He was your first boyfriend," Lilah guessed.

"No. Actually, yes, I suppose. I bet calling someone my boyfriend in grade school doesn't count." Angie gave a sigh. "I was so awkward. I met Manny after I enlisted. He bought me a drink at All Guns Blazing. That's why I'm not drinking *there*." She shook her head, more to herself as if she was forgiving her lack of strength. "I couldn't... Not that this isn't a nice bar," she added hastily looking up at Lilah, eyes wide.

Lilah chuckled as she waved a hand. "No offense taken, sweetie. You wait here a second. I'll be right back."

Angie watched curiously as Lilah made her way out

from behind the bar, and into the back corner of the row of booths.

At the back booth, a woman was drinking alone. Her long hair fell over her shoulders, and she wore a long coat and heavy boots. Despite the clothes, Angie could see that she was smiling. She spoke to Lilah easily, as if they knew each other.

She looked *familiar*...

Lilah walked up the path between the bar and the booths, she came back to Angie and jerked her head toward the corner. "Come on, there's someone I want you to meet."

Angie followed the bartender, aware as she focused on her walking that she'd had a lot to drink. She stumbled slightly, and had to focus hard on where her feet were to make sure she didn't end up in a heap.

When she got to the table, she took another look at the woman's face and put a hand up to her open mouth.

The lady looking up at her was Ranger *Two*.

Tabitha smiled at Angie. To Angie's surprise, the smile wasn't hard-edged or arrogant. It was almost mischievous.

"Take a seat, Angie," Tabitha suggested, waving a hand at the other side of the booth. When Angie's eyes widened, Tabitha tapped her skull. "My EI knows who you are."

I only said I knew her name, Achronyx commented in Tabitha's mind. His voice was prickly.

And her military record. She'll tell us whatever else we need to know, I'm sure.

It looks like she was next of kin for a Lieutenant Commander Manuel Fernandez. He died three months ago on the Recalcitrant.

See, that's more than we knew to start with. Tabitha wanted to roll her eyes at Achronyx. *It's obvious why Lilah wants us to talk with her, then.*

You're making an assumption.

Doesn't matter, because I'm also right, and you're being an ass.

Angie stood frozen until Lilah ushered her to the edge of the booth and pushed a bit to sit her down. Even then, it was all Angie could do to clutch her beer and not spill it everywhere.

Ranger Two. *She was talking with Ranger Two.*

"So," Tabitha began as Lilah disappeared to help a new customer. "Lilah tells me you need to hear one of my tales, and that maybe I need to tell it again." She took a swallow of her own beer, eyes focused on another time and place. "And maybe I do," she murmured, almost to herself.

Angie looked up to confirm with Lilah, but she was gone. "One of *your* stories?"

Tabitha nodded, thinking before looking Angie in her eyes. "I lost someone very close to me," she explained. "What happened after... Well, you can judge for yourself."

Angie took a sip of her beer, mostly to have something to do with her hands. It was hard not to be nervous under Tabitha's direct and self-assured gaze.

Tabitha considered, and started in a place Angie didn't expect. "I didn't start out as a fighter, you know."

"No?" Angie observed the easy way Tabitha wore her clothes, and at the way she held herself. This woman was a warrior, of that she had no doubt—regardless of the stories that were told around the *Meredith Reynolds*. She would have guessed that Tabitha had always been that way.

"Not at all. I was born on Earth, in Buenos Aires." Tabitha smiled. "How old are you?"

"Twenty-five." It was her silver birthday later this month, and... Angie swallowed. She knew Manny had already been planning something for her, even months ago.

She didn't know how she could face a birthday without him.

Tabitha saw all this in her shoulders, her posture, and her eyes. Despite everything, Tabitha *did* know what it felt like to need privacy while grieving. After Shin had died...

Well, she would be reliving it soon enough as she told Angie the tale.

"I was a street kid," Tabitha explained. "Not...homeless, exactly. I was a hacker—a real geek, let me tell you—and I got on the wrong side of someone very powerful. I went off on my own so that they wouldn't find my parents and siblings. I was hiding out, just trying to survive, when Bethany Anne found me."

You mean, when you were pulling off a heist in a bank, and she rescued the bank?

Shut up, Achronyx.

"And she wanted you to be a fighter?" Angie asked.

"No. Yes." Tabitha waved a hand. "It's not really impor-tant. I just meant to say, I think it will be helpful for the story if you realize I wasn't *always* a warrior. I didn't come from a family who knew about that stuff. When one of my comrades died, I didn't know how to handle it. Does that make sense?"

"I never would have guessed." Angie glanced at Tabitha almost shyly. "You look like you were born to your role."

"Most people would agree with you." Tabitha snickered.

"Except Hirotoshi and perhaps Ryu. Hirotoshi might feel otherwise with as much shit as I give him."

"But you learned," Angie countered. "You got through it. Right?"

"Yes." Tabitha nodded. She recognized Angie's drive to overcome this, and she respected it. "You see, it's *easy* to get lost in ourselves when we lose someone."

Angie gave a bitter smile. "I don't think there's much to get lost in. Manny had everything—looks, personality. He could cook. He was a good leader. He always found the perfect gifts for a birthday or a…a damned *Tuesday*. I don't know what he ever saw in me."

"What did Bethany Anne see in me?" Tabitha asked.

A criminal, I'm sure..

I said shut UP, Achronyx. Tabitha sent back, exasperated.

Angie sighed, clearly not convinced, but Tabitha refused to let it go. "Manny picked you for a reason. Right now you feel like doing nothing because you can't think of what else to do, but that's a crappy way to see yourself. When you get up in your head, thinking you have nothing beyond sadness or revenge or any of that, it *eats* away at you. I nearly lost myself. I don't want you to make the same mistake."

Angie looked at her. "I don't think—"

She stopped when she saw Tabitha's hand go up. "Let me tell you my story," Tabitha suggested. "I think Lilah's right, maybe you *need* to hear it."

A man with brown hair and lively black eyes turned around, the noise causing Tabitha then Angie to look over as he returned the look from his stool at the bar. "Do we get to hear the story again?"

"Hey, George." Tabitha lifted her beer. "Sure. Pull up a chair if you want."

"Hell yeah, I want." George dragged a chair from another table and sat next to Angie, holding out his hand. "Hi. George Danvers."

Confused, she reached over. "Angie." She replied, shaking his hand.

"Hey, Dan!" George hollered. "Kelly! Tabitha's telling the story again!"

Tabitha rolled her eyes with good humor as there were shouts from elsewhere in the bar. A few other people pulled over chairs of their own and settled down to listen.

"So you've told this before?" Angie asked.

"A few times," Tabitha admitted cagily.

"A *few* times." George shook his head. "Tons. And we still love hearing it. Why, it's practically an institution around here—of course, it's never the same story twice."

Tabitha took a sip of beer and gave them a little smile. "I tell the parts of it people need to hear each time."

"Uh-huh," George gave Angie a meaningful smile. "Anyway, settle in, you're gonna have a great time."

"All right," Tabitha said. "So, here's how I dealt with my first loss…"

Yoll Quadrant, QBSS *Meredith Reynolds*, Never Submit-Never Surrender Bar

"Perhaps you've heard of the Tontos?" Tabitha asked Angie.

The woman's eyes narrowed, and those watching stayed quiet. "Are they… They follow you, yes?"

"That's a very loose term for it." Tabitha chuckled. "If you mean, do they follow my orders, then yes. If you mean, do they follow my orders respectfully and to the letter? The answer is definitely *no*."

The people nearby snickered. A man was pulling up another chair, and he gave Angie a grin and a nod. His brown hair was cut fairly long and fell across his forehead in a long sweep, and his eyes had a hint of green to them. He had an open, easy manner about him that she liked.

"The Tontos are absolutely loyal," he explained to Angie. "Don't get the idea that they would ever disobey a direct order or betray their Lady Kemosabe."

"No one calls me that anymore," Tabitha interjected, and he eyed her. "Ok, other than them."

"It's such a lovely term for a delicate, feminine flower." He grinned at her.

Tabitha frowned at the guy. "Terrence, I will slap you into next week if you keep annoying me."

Terrence transferred his smile to Angie and stuck out his hand. "As you'll have guessed, I'm Terrence. You are?"

"Angie." She looked around at the crowd that was gathering. "I've been told I'm about to hear a story."

"Oh, it's legendary," he assured her. "I'll go get another round for everyone. The usual? George? Margie? Lady Kemosabe?" At the flash in Tabitha's eyes, he stuck up his hands and backed off. "I mean Tabitha. I'm going, I'm going."

Angie smiled after him. He had the same way about him that Manny'd had, making connections between people easily and naturally. When he was around, she had always felt that the world made sense and that there wasn't anything scary about it at all.

"Terrence is a good guy," Tabitha admitted. "Just a pain in the ass when he starts in on the Lady Kemosabe crap. Good drinking buddy, though. You ever played beer pong?"

"I…" Angie wondered if she was about to be asked to join a drinking game. Her stomach flipped at the mere thought of it, and she clapped a hand over her mouth.

"Never mind," Tabitha said hastily. "And remember, if you have to hurl," she pointed to the empty chair, "do it on Terrence."

Angie busted out laughing, and Tabitha grinned. She

was glad Terrence was here to set Angie at ease. Like a lot of people, Angie was having trouble getting past her awe at meeting the famous Ranger Two.

Hopefully, by the end of this Angie would see that she and Tabitha weren't so different—and that there was a way through grief, no matter how unlikely it seemed now.

"Anyway, the Tontos came to be in service to Bethany Anne back in an operation a long time ago. Let's just say the group they were a part of was given the option to join Bethany Anne's cause, and most of them did choose to. We got paired up and have been fighting together ever since."

"While Hirotoshi tries to turn Ranger Two into a lady," Terrence explained, coming back with his hands full of glasses. He set them down carefully and looked back at the bar. "See? I got them all!"

"You always say that," Lilah called from behind the group somewhere. "But it's only a matter of time until you drop one!"

"She has no faith," Terrence explained to Angie. He set another drink in front of her. "Best keep drinking. You're falling behind."

Angie laughed and took a sip of her beer.

"So the Tontos and I were together for a while back on Earth, but not so much here in Yollin space," Tabitha explained. "We came upon some Skaine ships—slavers. They knew I was looking for slavers. They knew they weren't supposed to be there. We lured them onto another ship from the *Achronyx*. The Tontos were on it, and they were able to keep the Skaines from sensing them on scanners—one of the benefits of their set of 'upgrades.'"

She smiled wryly. The profusion of nanites on Earth

hadn't been at all controlled or deliberate. It had been a hacked-together process, and Michael had developed the best rules he could to cope with it. There had been many drawbacks, such as the inability to tolerate sunlight for most who had the vampiric version of the nanos.

And while some, like the Tontos, had come out of the changes with their minds intact, the Nosferatu had been more plentiful, and a menace.

It was fascinating to know the changes and be able to control the process. What had once been close to torture was now painless and could be directed to produce specific results.

It was what gave Tabitha her abilities, and sometimes she wondered if she would have been able to withstand the conversion in the way Michael and many of the others had been forced to endure it.

Barnabas wouldn't even speak of it. When Tabitha thought of the fortitude it would have taken to withstand the whispers that spoke of an end to the pain, a release from agony…

It gave her more of an appreciation for Shin, and she felt her grief well up again.

"The Tontos fought well," she swallowed her bit of pain, "but the captain panicked and undocked the ships, and the gravity went nuts. Shin was crushed by debris during the fight." Her hands tightened, and the glass in her hands cracked. Tabitha swore, moving a hand so the glass didn't cut it. "That always happens." Tabitha looked toward the bar. "Lilah?"

"Not again." But Lilah sounded good-natured as she brought another beer and swept the glass and spilled beer away with expert speed. "Keep talking. And don't break any more glasses!"

"I won't," Tabitha called, moving a hand down and then across her chest. "Promise."

She took a long pause as she tried to find the fortitude to tell the rest of the story, and the others waited patiently. Tabitha had told it a fair number of times, but only when there was someone who needed to hear it. Anyone who saw her tell it knew how much it cost her.

Lilah was right that Tabitha was not done grieving this loss. In some ways, she had come to terms with the fact that she would never stop, but she did not fear that as much as she once had.

She hoped that was the lesson Angie would take from the story.

"When I came back," Tabitha continued finally, "I was in a black hole of grief. The rest of my friends, my Tontos, supported me as best they could, but how do you get support from five Japanese vampires who've seen centuries of life when you are less than fifty years old yourself? I was *such* a baby then."

Angie, who at twenty-five was thinking she was very old and worldly, blinked in surprise. How could anyone who was fifty think they were a baby?

Angie leaned forward. "What did the Tontos say about grieving, given that they were so old? I mean, they must have lost people before. What did they say the best way to get through it was?"

"Hmm." Tabitha considered Angie's question.

The truthful answer, of course, was that the Tontos had given her a lot of sensible advice about how what happened to Shin wasn't her fault, and how sometimes people died in battle, and how Shin had been glad to have the life he had.

The even *more* truthful answer was that none of that advice had helped at all. To lose someone so suddenly was something that the mind couldn't make sense of, and grief wasn't something that followed any rules about how to behave.

The advice had been useless. In the end, it had been their companionship and accountability that helped—the fact that they cared enough to try to make her feel better, and they stuck with her after it happened.

That, and grieving in her own way. Nothing Tabitha could say would make things better for Angie.

"Why don't I tell the story first," she suggested, "and then if you still have questions, we'll go over any lost wisdom from the Tontos? Hopefully, between my fuck-ups and what they did to help me, you'll be all set."

Angie nodded. Tabitha sounded halfway between exasperated and fond when she talked about the Japanese vampires, as if they were troublesome older brothers who were a pile of annoyances but still deeply loved.

She nodded and settled in to listen.

"Now, the problem, of course," Tabitha confided, "is that my nanites clean up my blood, and it is terribly hard to get drunk..."

"Yeah," Lilah called from at the bar. "Not that she didn't try!"

The others chuckled, and some knowing looks between them suggested that there had been a lot of nights of drinking games—fairly epic ones if it was nearly impossible for Tabitha to get drunk.

"So, if drinking didn't work." Angie looked around, seeking confirmation, "and the Tontos' help didn't work, how did you deal with it? What did you do?"

"Killed a lot of Skaines," Terrence answered succinctly.

"Spoiler alert."

"Ow!" He rubbed the back of his head.

Tabitha had slapped Terrence on the back of the head. She clearly wasn't trying to hurt him, but *damn*, Tabitha was lightning-fast, and he hadn't gotten out of the way in time.

"Serves you right." Tabitha took a sip of her beer and glared at him.

"She's here for the journey, not the destination. I'm just setting the stage. It's the movie's trailer, if you will." Terrence leaned in to grin at Angie, raising his eyebrows as he made a rectangle with his fingers. "Picture it: Tabitha in skintight armor, two Jean Dukes pistols holstered on her legs, knives sheathed next to them." He spread his hands apart, looking both ways. "Blood *everywhere*."

Surprised, Angie gave a snort of laughter.

"That's pretty accurate, actually." Tabitha tapped a finger on the table. "I punched a lot of them to death."

Angie stopped mid-drink. She looked at all of them, trying to decide if Tabitha was serious.

The beer started talking. Well, Angie hoped it was the beer. "So you want me to kill a lot of Skaines to get over Manny?" she asked finally.

Tabitha looked wistful for a moment. "That would be

great." She nodded. "But no. It was wrong, and I shouldn't have done it."

"But I thought the Skaines... I thought you... I'm confused." Angie shook her head. "These were Skaine slavers, right? I mean. They were Skaines. Why *shouldn't* you deal with them?"

Tabitha sighed. "When you are a Ranger, it's more complicated than just killing slavers. Bethany Anne has never been one for meaningless bureaucracy and paper-work, but there are reasons to be discerning about who you kill."

Terrence leaned in once more to stage-whisper, "It's good to hear our resident Ranger admit that there might be reasons for not engaging in wanton murder." He looked from her to Tabitha and back.

Angie shot him a grin, and even Tabitha smiled in a distracted way.

"You see, I set out to teach the Skaines a lesson," the Ranger admitted finally, "and since I have a long life, I intended to personally teach them *all* a lesson." She lifted her drink. "I was a bit of a loose cannon."

"What happens when...well, when that happens?" Angie asked. "Did Ranger One intervene?"

Tabitha glared at Terrence, who had his glass up and was drinking, so she answered the question. "Not exactly. He'd seen it all before." Tabitha rolled her glass on the table, lost in thought. "The first thing we have to learn is to be patient with ourselves. None of my friends, with centuries or a millennium on their side, told me to just tough it out. They were there to pick up the pieces and help me—while making sure I didn't do anything too stupid."

"Like the time you told that Skaine battleship to fuck off," Terrence piped up, his glass just touching the table.

"That's a story for another time," Tabitha retorted. "So, I decide I'm going to take down the Skaines in a one-Ranger effort to clean up the Universe…"

"How did that work?" Angie asked. She looked around at all of them, still wide-eyed.

"About as well as one would think. One Ranger versus a whole race of people on multiple planets breeding like bunnies." Tabitha looked up a moment, her lips folded between her teeth. "I consider it a tie," Tabitha finally answered with a smile. "Since they hate my ass, we are on an even footing."

"They *respect* you, not hate you," Lilah interjected. She was clearing up glasses, and she paused, considering. "No, that's not right. They hate you, too."

Everyone chuckled once more.

"Speak softly and carry a large stick?" Angie asked.

"Oh, hell no!" Tabitha shook her head. "Yell at those sonsabitches and have a big-assed Etheric Empire super-dreadnought behind you."

"Tabitha doesn't do quiet," Terrence told Angie. He smiled at her as the rest murmured in agreement.

"Never," Tabitha agreed. "So, I decided the first thing I needed to do, was find some snitches—"

Angie was confused. She really wished she had more of her mental faculties. "What's a snitch?"

Tabitha blinked. "What, you… *Wow*, what are they

teaching you young'uns nowadays? A snitch is a person who will give you information on the side. They will 'snitch' on their friends for a price. An informant. No one *likes* snitches, but in this case, I had a feeling they might be useful."

Tabitha leaned forward with a conspiratorial grin. Now that she had gotten past speaking directly about Shin's death, she was able to look back on the story with more humor.

After all, one's misadventures are always viewed with better humor from a distance.

"So I decide to find some snitches," she repeated. "We were going to use them to track down the Skaines—any we could find—and, well, make an example of them. I was done playing nice. I wasn't going to let them get away with what they'd done to Shin..."

Memory took over, and though she could still hear her voice speaking in the back corner of the bar, she was far away, both in years and distance, in the landing bay of Farha Station, far out in the Imdali system, two Gates away from the Etheric Empire...

"This...is just fucking *weird*," Tabitha commented. She tapped the holster of her Jean Dukes and looked around, her face showing both confusion and repulsion simultaneously.

Farha Station hadn't been designed for humans. Everything was slightly, subtly proportioned *wrong*, so that you began to feel like your whole reality was off. It was like being a doll in the wrong-sized dollhouse.

"I agree, Kemosabe." Hirotoshi looked around, eyes alert. "Perhaps we should find another location. Somewhere more suited to...reliable people."

"You mean we should find another plan," Tabitha retorted, her arms crossed on her chest. "You don't think snitches are a good place to start."

"No." Hirotoshi shook his head. "I do not. Snitches, by their very nature, lack honor *and* loyalty. How are we to trust what they say?"

Tabitha smiled sweetly as she lifted a finger. "One, we need to find Skaines, and two, Skaines don't have honor or loyalty, so it makes sense that the people who snitch on them wouldn't either."

Hirotoshi considered this and sighed. "That doesn't make any damned sense."

Tabitha looked at Hirotoshi, shocked that he had cursed, before replying with the appropriate amount of respect. At least, appropriate coming from her. "Shut up and stop informing me why this amazing idea is possibly a bit short," she answered grumpily. "I say we're sticking around until we find a snitch and find some Skaines."

Hirotoshi raised an eyebrow. "Yes, Kemosabe."

Her face looked like she had just bitten into a lemon and found it way too tart. "Don't say 'Yes, Kemosabe' in that disapproving way. That's just not nice."

He raised his eyebrow again. "*Of course* not, Kemosabe."

"Oh, for fuck's sake!" Tabitha threw up her hands, wanting to bitch to the ceiling, for all of the good it would do. She pointed to the two of them. "You know what? We're going to go find a bar because bars are where there are a lot of people, and we can probably find a snitch. Even if we can't, we can find a drink, and I'll have another shot at getting drunk."

"This isn't going to work," Ryu interjected. "However, I will support the idea wholeheartedly if you can think of a way we can bet on this." He followed Tabitha. "What about we bet you can't get drunk? You try drinking like you are a fish, and then—"

"*NO!*" Tabitha waved a hand, remembering the last time Ryu had pulled this trick on her. "No Hilashin rum. Those fucking impurities gave me a damned headache for half an hour before the nanos finally kicked in." She looked back to see Ryu smiling. "Damn, sometimes you can be such a dick."

"Nickie, time to shake a leg!" Meredith's call in her audio implant jolted Nickie out of the account her aunt was painting from the past.

What is it?

We're docking at the spaceport. Thought you might like to know.

With a dramatic sigh, Nickie shuffled off the undersize bed still with her boots on and stretched, closing the file for now. Moments later she emerged from the room and headed for the bridge to meet Grim.

Rebus Quadrant, Minerva Trading Outpost

Docking at the outpost went smoothly enough. Nothing out of the ordinary happened, and the docking officers seemed disinclined to ask any questions other than the basics—ship's name, captain, docking requirements, reason for docking at the outpost—and it went smoothly.

It seemed somewhat impossible, considering how *unsmoothly* everything else had gone recently. Nickie was willing to assume it was Meredith's doing, but the EI offered no indication either way.

Nickie and Grim stepped optimistically from the airlock into the docking tube, and they followed the gritty gray tube to some stairs. It was a few models old, and it creaked as they walked. Nickie had seen even older models in worse condition stand up to cannon fire. Still, she suppressed the urge to jump just to get the tube to sway.

They stepped down the stairs at the end of the tube, and they both spared a moment to glance around. Nickie could already see navigation notes appearing in the corner of her eye, though they faded into visual white noise as she let her attention slide past them for the time being.

Even from the distance of the docking bay, the noise and the bustle of the rest of the outpost was still audible. Nickie could hear shouting, even if she couldn't make out most of the words.

She was willing to bet, though, that most of the shouting wasn't swearing like it would have been back on the ship.

But they were there to fix that! Maybe. Possibly. It wasn't her top priority.

"You go in whatever direction you need to go," she instructed Grim after a moment as she turned toward him. He paused, already a few steps away, as if he had already been in the process of doing just that. Nickie carried on, regardless. "I'll go this way. We'll meet back here once we've got everything we need. Two-and-a-half hours. Or sooner, if you really want to be a good friend."

"Bossy," Grim deadpanned, but he flashed a brief thumbs-up in agreement before he started walking away in earnest. He disappeared into the crowd in just a few seconds.

Finally, Nickie actually turned her attention to the data being fed to her. She took a moment to figure out where she was in relation to the details Meredith was giving her before she started moving at a spritely jog. Her boots thumped on the corrugated metal that made up the floor of the docking bay.

Maybe she would find a replacement for her shoes while she was there.

Keep dreaming, Meredith informed her blandly.

If she cared at all about Nickie's ruined shoes—astoundingly unlikely, admittedly—she was hiding it very well.

You are such a buzzkill.

Nickie would not admit to pouting, but it was all right. She didn't actually need to admit to it for it to be obvious.

CHAPTER 4 NICKIE

The Minerva Outpost might as well have been paradise, compared to what Nickie had become accustomed to recently.

She felt like she had been thrown into a bakery after becoming used to eating only dry crusts. A chain bakery where everything just tasted sweet instead of having any sort of flavor, maybe, but a bakery nonetheless. It was an upgrade.

I'm fairly sure someone who only ate bread but suddenly switched to cupcakes would get sick, Meredith reported flatly.

Nickie found it hard to tell if she was serious.

That much sugar all at once would be horrible for someone whose body was unaccustomed to it.

Nickie was willing to assume she wasn't. So much for EI logic.

No one likes a pedant, Nickie informed her.

Meredith didn't have a response ready for that, so Nickie ignored her. Because really, if Meredith wanted to pick apart every single metaphor she came up with, Nickie didn't need to play along.

Nickie picked up the pace, weaving around people and ducking under stray arms. She kept up her speed until she got to one of the main shopping areas. It was lit in every shade of neon, the signs of the shops that lined the walls almost entirely drowning out the lighting on the ceiling that loomed far above the cavernous area.

There wasn't an inch of wall space that wasn't occupied by some sort of store, and there were *even more* stores. They were stacked on top of each other, lifts and escalators leading to the walkway that passed the front of the second row of shopfronts. Even so, that wasn't all of them. Carts and tents and stands were propped up all over the floor in the center of the room. It looked like chaos at first glance, and Nickie couldn't help but wonder just how many people had been trampled in the crush. At second glance, though, she could see the order of it. Each pop-up shop took up only a very specific amount of space, and though there were no lines on the floor, she could recognize the grid system they were set up on.

Even so, she could easily imagine someone getting trampled in an emergency, and it would be a nightmare if she needed to make a sudden break for an exit.

There was cosmetic tech, home appliances, luxury tech, holoconsoles and wrist holos, tools and upgrades of every shape, size, and utility, real estate depots, cars, and even civilian ships.

And that was just what she could see from where she was standing.

She looked farther up the walls, shading her eyes with

her hand as she did so. She knew the outpost had residential units—not many, and mostly they belonged to the shop owners and their families—but she had yet to catch a glimpse of one.

She had to squint past the light to see them. Two-thirds of the way up the towering walls there was a broader walkway, where she could make out the doors to the apartments. She could even see a few people on the walkway, coming and going.

She had to wonder just how good the insulation was to block out all the noise from the floor below.

Meredith sent a tiny shock down her spine, jolting her back to the present before that thought could go to any horrible places.

I wasn't even going there. You went there first, and that makes you the pervert. Nickie scowled at nothing in particular and took a furtive look around to make sure no one had seen her jump for no apparent reason.

A vendor eyed her warily, then very deliberately turned away to talk to someone else. Likely he either assumed her to be high or a thief, and she folded her arms over her chest and harrumphed at the assumption. It wasn't as if she were the weirdest person he had ever seen. Such a busy outpost had to get its own fair share of whack jobs and crazies.

She shook her head briefly, yanking her attention back to the moment at hand before she could get too distracted.

She walked farther into the room to get away from him, passing a darkened shopfront with flavored smoke drifting out of it. The urge to go inside reared its head, and she paused outside the entryway. Music and conversation in low tones drifted out. With an effort of will, Nickie turned away from the entrance and kept walking before Meredith could shock her again. She had no doubt that the EI would do so. She nearly tripped over one of the carrier bots that would help her carry things once she started purchasing. The hands-free shopping carts dogged her heels like puppies, and Nickie side-stepped them both.

She just...needed to find everything on the list Meredith had given her.

I could tell you where to go, Meredith pointed out.

Rather than smug, she simply sounded matter-of-fact.

I have a map of this entire outpost, with a guide on what shop sells what.

Nickie only remembered at the last instant not to physically wave the suggestion off. People already thought she was weird, and she didn't need to make it worse. The last thing she needed was security coming to escort her to the checkpoint or back to the docking bay.

I can handle it, she insisted, planting her hands on her hips as she kept walking. Half the fun of shopping was seeing what was there, after all. There was always time for window-shopping.

Granted, she couldn't say she would complain if the entire outpost was just a little less damnably loud. Like, just half a notch.

Vendors shouted back and forth, some trying to attract customers and others just trying to be heard over the noise as they bartered. Nickie sighed, deciding then that she would just get used to the noise; let it wash over her until she didn't even notice it anymore. She wondered if Meredith might have an app for that.

She turned in a circle to get a quick look at everything

around her, ignoring the odd looks she got from the rest of the crowd. She had hardly been at the outpost for twenty minutes, and already there were so many things she wanted to get her hands on.

She had seen better in the past, of course. Back in the Federation, the tech itself probably would have laughed at the outpost. But compared to what she had become accustomed to during her sabbatical, she wasn't going to complain.

Sabbatical, Meredith repeated dubiously. *Is that what we're calling it now? Like it was an optional thing and you were always planning to get back to your duties? This is certainly news to me. I'll have to update my databanks with this revelation.*

Nickie heaved an aggrieved sigh, her shoulders rising and falling with the motion. She ignored the new slew of odd looks it garnered her.

Meredith?' She sighed, because evidently it was quite possible to sigh inside one's own head given enough determination. She wasn't surprised. Rhinoceros-like determination had gotten her some surprising results in all sorts of situations.

Yes? The EI sounded innocent. Nickie didn't buy it for a second.

Shut up.

There was no response after that. It probably wasn't a win, but Nickie was willing to count it as one for the time being. She nodded once to herself, shoved her hands in her pockets, and turned on her heel to go pick out some cheap housebots. No way in hell was she cleaning that entire ship with her two hands.

Fuel cells? Check.
Console covers? Check.
Wireless network extenders? Check.
Holobrighteners? Check.
Auxiliary radiation dampeners? Check.
Shielding capacitors? Check.
A high-quality deck of playing cards? Check.

She had gotten all those, plus various other odds and ends that Meredith assured her were missing from the ship and would be helpful, even if they wouldn't make or break any situations that she could predict.

As Nickie mentally went through a checklist, a literal one appeared at the edge of her vision. She squinted at it skeptically before turning her attention from it. She glanced at her borrowed pair of bots, dutifully holding everything except the dampeners and the capacitors.

The vendor in front of her drummed his fingers on the counter. "As I asked, is the price—"

"It's fine." Nickie cut him off and sighed. It was a bit pricey actually, but she had negotiated as low a price as she would be able to get without being tossed out of the shop. "Does it include delivery to the ship?" She glanced at the carrier bots again. "They aren't that big," she stated, and her gaze traveled to the capacitors and the dampeners, which were all nearly the same size as the bots.

The vendor paused and turned that over for a moment before he nodded once, slow and decisive. "Fine," he agreed, drumming his fingers once again, his eyes narrowing slightly. "You pay for half up front, though," he added as if he thought Nickie was just going to karate-kick him into unconsciousness at the dock and run off with the supplies.

She couldn't say the thought hadn't crossed her mind, but she decided to feel offended. With a roll of her eyes, she folded her arms over her chest and slumped her weight to one side. "Yeah, yeah, fine." She huffed. "Let's just get it over with. I have places to be."

The vendor turned his console to face her so she could type in her payment information, and as soon as she tapped the Accept button, he got much more tractable. With an almost cloying smile he bade her have a pleasant rest of her day, and as she turned to start heading back to the docking bay, the vendor called assurances that her order would be there to meet her in perfect condition before she even knew it.

She figured he meant to wait until she was out of earshot before he started hollering at his assistants to get everything together, but he was out of luck there. Nickie probably would have been able to hear him from the other side of the outpost what with all her enhancements, including the additional ones that had kicked in since the Skaine scuffle.

"How charming," she grumbled under her breath, shoving her hands into her pockets. "What else do we need?" she asked thin air, slowing to a halt again.

Meredith was quick to answer. *Even as augmented as you are, you and your cook—*

Chef, Nickie corrected absentmindedly.

Cannot crew an entire ship on your own, Meredith finished

her initial point. *You are going to need other people to help run the ship, since utilizing the ship's existing crew seems to be out of the question.*

I'm pretty sure they'd rather throw me out the airlock, Nickie agreed, and she started heading back toward the main shopping area. It would take time for the auxiliary radiation dampeners and the shield capacitors to be delivered, and she wasn't going to shed any tears if she was a bit late to meet the vendor at the docking bay. She turned to the two bots dogging her, keyed in the location of the ship, and sent them off. Hopefully Grim would be there to let them on board, but even if he wasn't, she knew they had loss-prevention programming. They could take care of themselves.

In the meantime, she had an idea of where she could start looking for the right kinds of people.

I have a bad feeling about this, Meredith grumbled.

CHAPTER 5 NICKIE

Grim glanced over his shoulder one last time as he walked away from the ship, to see Nickie's back disappearing in the other direction. He kept moving at a lope, and after a couple of minutes before he found a board declaring, YOU ARE HERE with a red spot on a map. He gave it a brief scan, then turned and started in the direction that seemed the most likely to be helpful.

He took his time, picking up a bot to help him carry everything as he selected supplies. The galley's appliances were fine and he was mostly after food, but even so, he wound up selecting a few knives to let the bot carry as well. He just couldn't help himself.

He browsed freely, though he avoided every vendor who seemed intent on force-feeding samples to anyone who passed. Even as a chef, sometimes these things were just a bit too much.

The outpost made all the canned goods back on the ship seem even less appealing, he mused to himself.

Despite his efforts though, he still retained the niggling feeling that Nickie would continue to be just as happy eating cold beans out of a can even once the kitchen was fully restocked.

He sighed to himself and refused to dwell on it. Instead, he dwelt on whether he should aim for quality or quantity before ultimately deciding on the latter. It wouldn't matter all that much if the food was fancy if there wasn't enough of it to go around, and Grim liked to think he was the practical sort.

Not that he didn't still *admire* all the higher-quality foods, appliances, and cutlery. Staring was after all free, even if the vendors fancied themselves as Venetian merchants.

Even taking his time, Grim was pretty sure he had plenty to spare once he turned to head back to the ship. Truth be told, he was sort of glad. As dismal as the ship still was and as uncomfortable as the Skaines locked behind almost every door made it, the ship at least just smelled like...a ship. Metal, cleaner, and manufactured atmosphere.

The outpost, by contrast, smelled like every single food Grim could think of, all at the same time.

Suffice it to say he was getting more than a little nauseated, and he put a little extra pep in his step as he headed back to the docking bay.

When he made it back to the ship there were two bots waiting, laden with what he had to assume were Nickie's purchases. There was also one impatient vendor off to the side, alternately pacing and tapping his feet.

Grim ignored the vendor for the time being—not his problem—and ushered Nickie's bots and his own onto the ship. He escorted two of them to storage for lack of an idea of where else to send them, and they trundled back to the docking bay once they were done carrying things. The third followed Grim to the galley, and it too made its way back off of the ship once it was done depositing his goods.

Grim took his time putting things away, using it as an exercise to better acquaint himself with the layout of the place. To say it lacked character was being polite—gray, gray, and more gray—but it was functional and of a decent size.

The ship seemed too quiet just then. Although he knew exactly how many Skaines were locked on board, it didn't change the fact that there was no one in the corridors and, for all intents and purposes, he and Nickie were the only actual crew members at that point. Talk about a skeleton crew.

And with no one around, it felt as if the galaxy had suddenly gotten very small. He pushed the thought from his mind and focused on putting things away. He could deal with awkward quiet.

BANG!

He jumped and nearly hit his head on the cupboard he was stocking when there was a resounding *bang* from the other side of the wall in front of him. He scowled at it for a moment, then he grabbed a tin mug and thumped it against the wall in return.

"I'm going!" he shouted at the wall. "Calm your britches, or I'll take even longer!"

The ruckus on the other side of the wall only got louder, so Grim hammered the mug against the wall a few more times until at last the racket began to die down. He scowled balefully at the wall for a few seconds longer, just for good measure.

Finally, he heaved a sigh and turned away from the wall, instead facing the counter. He set the slightly dented mug down.

"Right. Food," he muttered to himself. "Because that's always fun when I've got someone breathing down my neck."

He shook his head and started gathering ingredients, his tone too cheerful by half as he assured himself, "Nothing out of the ordinary there, I guess. It'll be fine."

With that bit of admittedly weak assurance, he laid out the supplies and ingredients he would need and got to work. He had a lot of mouths to feed, after all, and none of them were patient or polite.

A datapad met the wall, and it sparked as the screen cracked and it clattered to the floor. When that had no effect, Slevin and Barqx instead hurled themselves at the wall, hammering at it and body-slamming it ineffectually. Across the room, Drell and Herz were slamming them-selves into the door as Grets tried shorting out the door controls, to no avail.

Standing near the back wall, Durq flinched every time

they made the walls rattle—as if there were any possibility of them doing any kind of lasting damage to the ship.

For a few seconds, everyone fell quiet as someone on the opposite side of the wall banged on it in return and shouted back. And then Krask stepped forward. He grabbed Slevin and Barqx by the backs of their necks and tossed them aside, and he lunged forward, head-butting the wall with all his might.

Not much happened, other than more pounding from whoever was on the opposite side. Durq stepped closer to the back wall regardless, his hands clasped to his chest as he fidgeted.

Still shaking his head to shake off the impact, Krask turned to peer slowly over his shoulder, his gaze locking on Durq. "Problem?" he wondered, feigning a casual tone without much luck.

"Wha... Uh, no. Nope." Durq shook his head quickly and dropped his hands to his sides. "Nothing like that. No problems here, no sirree."

Slowly, Krask grinned and turned the rest of the way around so he could take a step closer. "Are you sure about that?" he wondered, in a tone that was trying and failing to be mild. "You look like you aren't having the best time."

Durq's shoulders rounded as he shrank in on himself and his hands rose to resume fidgeting in front of his chest. He kept his eyes trained carefully on a spot just past Krask's shoulder. "It's, uh... It's nothing. I am a-okay."

"You should really look at someone when you're talking to them," Krask pointed out reasonably, taking another step closer. "It's rude not to. You might offend someone."

"Of course. You're right. Definitely." Durq darted a brief

glance at Krask's face, then looked back at the spot on the wall after meeting Krask's eyes for only the barest moment.

"Not quite what I meant," Krask replied, suddenly much closer as he cleared the last of the space between them to stand nose-to-nose with Durq. Durq nearly leapt out of his boots, and it was only a flinch at the last instant that kept him from accidentally head-butting Krask in the nose.

"Not good for all that much, are you?" Krask mused, seemingly to himself, though the other five Skaines in the room with them were clearly paying attention. Slevin and Barqx were even snickering, their hands in front of their faces.

Krask grinned again, toothy and broad. "But I guess you might come in handy if it takes too long for dinner to show up," he decided, giving Durq a once-over. "You look like you've got some meat on your bones."

Durq stumbled back two steps until he was wedged between a pair of cabinets. With one more laugh, Krask finally turned away to let him have some peace—not that it did much good at that point.

Durq cringed and sat down on the floor as the other six resumed throwing themselves at the wall like the galaxy's tiniest stampede. He was content to stay right where he was.

Rebus Quadrant, Minerva Trading Outpost

Nickie slowed to a halt in front of the same bar she had passed earlier. The music drifting out of it was different, though it was still just as smooth as before, and the smell of the flavored smoke still made her mouth water.

She shook her head quickly before she stepped inside. She was there for a reason. She had to stay on task.

It was dim inside, and the combination of smoke and the music made everything seem almost illicit even though nearly everyone inside was simply sitting and drinking. It didn't even look like any drug deals were going on under the tables. She supposed those were taking place in the docking bay. Ships and docking tubes were remarkably handy things to hide behind, after all.

She strolled over to the counter and took a seat, and a bartender was standing in front of her before Nickie could even lift a hand to flag one of them down. It was a brief matter to order a drink, though the bartender lingered once she set the glass down on the counter in front of Nickie.

"You after something other than just a drink?" the bartender ventured, folding her arms on the counter and leaning on them. "You've got that twitchy sort of look about you." She sounded a bit like she was revving up to kick Nickie out of the bar if she was up to anything untoward.

Nickie snorted indelicately and drained half of her glass in one swig. "Any idea where I can find some people who know something about ships?" she asked, leaning one elbow on the counter and propping her chin in her hand. "I'm a little short-staffed right now."

The bartender didn't even bother to hide the way she relaxed minutely at how tame the request turned out to be. She thought it over for a moment, then lifted a hand and pointed to one of the tables. "I would try him first," she answered, and then she listed two other names and pointed to nearby tables, quick enough that Nickie barely had time to make note of them. "Other than them, I can't help you."

Nickie saluted her with her glass and hopped down from the stool to head to the first table.

Are you sure this is the best place to try to pick up a functional crew member? Meredith wondered dubiously. *To my knowledge, there are places one can go that are dedicated to hiring such people.*

It'll be fine, Nickie assured her, and she threw back the last of her drink. *Just leave it to me.*

She came to a halt at the edge of the first table. The man seated there was attractive—tall, broad, and clearly accustomed to keeping himself in shape. There was a young woman practically sitting in his lap, running the tip of one finger in a circle on his chest as she simpered in his ear.

Nickie sat down across from them, set her empty glass down, perched both elbows on the table, and cupped her chin in both hands. "Hi there," she offered brightly as if there wasn't anywhere else in the world she was supposed to be. "I'm looking to hire a few new crew members on my ship. Heard you might be good for it."

His eyebrows rose slightly, and he waved off the girl draped over him. With a pout, she shoved herself away from the table and skulked away.

The man gave Nickie a once-over, slow and deliberate, before he licked his lips. "And what's the pay like for being part of your crew?" he asked. Nickie could feel her hackles rising already. He grinned slowly. "Trust me, I'm good enough to earn it."

"Egos get people shot out of the sky," Nickie informed

him, her tone almost sickeningly pleasant. "You might want to keep an eye on that."

He scoffed. "Give me half an hour and I can prove it."

Frankly, Nickie already knew she didn't even want to give him half a minute. Instead, she asked, "Got any credentials I can see? Just to prove that your ego isn't smoke and mirrors."

He grunted in irritation but presented an engineering license. Nickie squinted at it, scrutinizing it carefully. It was definitely him and it didn't look fake, but she had never heard of him. So really, how good could he be if he hadn't even made a name for himself?

She flicked the license back at him like a paper football, and he fumbled to catch it.

With a tight smile, Nickie assured him, "I'll be in touch."

She got to her feet and pushed herself away from the table with more force than was strictly necessary, moving on to the next target the bartender had pointed out to her.

The next target turned out to be *two* targets; a pair of twin girls sat at the table. They listened to Nickie's pitch with a cheerful sort of patience and then they launched almost simultaneously into a rambling speech about their skills and assets, speaking over each other so loudly and so quickly that Nickie recoiled slightly. She could barely make out a word of what they were saying until they finished, with one of the girls saying, "And the first four blew up pretty spectacularly, but two of those at least made it out of dry dock, and the fifth one held up pretty well for a few weeks!"

Nickie stared at them blankly for a long moment, then

got to her feet and walked away without a word. Behind her, one of them called, "Okay, bye-bye!"

Nickie started walking faster. She shot the bartender a beseeching look as she hurried away from the table, but the bartender simply shrugged unsympathetically and went back to wiping down the counter.

Rude.

Nickie could practically feel Meredith gearing up to say something, so she cut the EI off with a preemptive, *Not a word. I still have this under control.*

Rebus Quadrant, Minerva Trading Outpost, Aboard the *Penitent Granddaughter*

Occasionally, Grim wished he had more arms. Maybe just another pair. Or two extra pairs, at most. He wasn't asking for a lot. It would just be convenient sometimes, he reflected as he hammered the dented mug against the wall to get the Skaines in the next room to be quiet again. He immediately dragged his attention back to the pot on the stove in front of him.

The shouting and the thumping next door went quiet for a few seconds, but it started up again almost immediately. With an exasperated, "Gaaaaah," Grim tried to tune it out. He snatched up a container of…

He squinted at the label.

He couldn't tell what it said. But all the ingredients he had picked had *looked* familiar, and when he pulled off the lid and took a tentative sniff, it *smelled* familiar. So with some trepidation, he tipped a couple teaspoons of what gave every indication of simply being red pepper into the boiling pot.

Nothing happened at first, so he put the lid back on the jar and put it aside. Then the contents of the pot burst into spectacular flames. With a yelp high-pitched enough that it could have shattered glass, Grim pulled the pot off of the burner and leapt away from it. His legs got tangled in a chair, and he went to the floor in a heap.

He kicked his way free of the chair and scrambled gracelessly back to his feet, and for a moment he just stared at the still-flaming pot before he started frantically searching for the lid. If he could suffocate it before it caught anything else in the kitchen on fire, all the better.

He cringed so hard it was very nearly audible when the fire alarm started to go off, a strobe light flashing rhythmically as a high-pitched siren whined unendingly. Grim paused in his search for a lid to put on the pot to instead throw a mug of water at the pot. As he suspected, though, it had little effect. He didn't really expect water to have much of an impact on the flames when the contents of the pot were mostly liquid.

The shouting in the room next door was getting louder, and he could hear it picking up in the room to the galley's other side and then across the hall. Soon enough it was so loud that Grim could scarcely hear himself think, and the idea of just letting the ship catch on fire suddenly became that much more tempting.

But no. No, he couldn't do that. He would just have to… do something else.

Chaos erupted ship-wide.

The Skaines in every room in every direction began shouting and arguing with all the door controls once the fire alarm started to go off. Krask seemed curiously unconcerned about it. Durq ducked farther back into his spot between the cabinets, but Krask's gaze fell on him anyway.

"You suppose the heat would be enough to cook this one?" he mused out loud, slow and mild, as he eyed Durq thoughtfully.

Barqx snickered and replied, "If you throw him in deep enough, it probably would."

Durq wedged himself even deeper into the corner and tried to pull one of the cabinets closer to close off the gap. It was firmly bolted to the floor, though, so it wasn't going anywhere.

Slowly, Krask started advancing toward him, one steady step at a time, as if he were being egged on by the sound of the siren and the shouting of every other Skaine down the corridor.

Durq whimpered and sat on the floor.

CHAPTER 6 NICKIE

Rebus Quadrant, Minerva Trading Outpost

With a mounting sense of dread, Nickie sat down at the third table that had been pointed out to her, practically slumping on it. The man across from her was older than she would have expected, but maybe age bred experience in his case.

He waited until Nickie finished explaining the specs of the *Granddaughter's* core and engine before he cut her off with a snap of his fingers.

"I've worked on plenty of those!" he assured her, and for a moment Nickie felt a spark of hope. "You've probably heard of some of them!" He started ticking them off on his fingers as he listed names. "The *Oglethorpe*, the *Wrassler*, the *Orange Marmaduke...*"

He kept listing ships, and true enough, Nickie recognized some of the names.

She had seen each and every one of them listed for sale

in scrap shops. Some of them had fallen out of the atmosphere pretty spectacularly.

Before Nickie could come up with a reason to excuse herself from the conversation, Meredith interrupted her chain of thought.

We have something of a situation back on the ship. I'm doing what I can to keep outpost security at bay, but you should return.

Nickie cleared her throat and told the old geezer, "You know, I don't think you're going to work out," and shrugged blithely. She got to her feet, and as soon as she turned away her face fell, exasperation creeping across her features.

Seriously? You can't handle it on your own?' Nickie griped at her as she stormed toward the door.

Not if you want the Skaines on board to survive.

There was a beat before Nickie pointed out slowly, *I mean, I'm not exactly their biggest fan.*

Nickie! Meredith snapped.

Nickie nearly leapt out of her boots and cast around quickly to make sure no one saw her jumping at shadows.

Don't yell at me, she groused in return.

But she picked up the pace.

Then get your sorry excuse for a behind back to your ship and handle this.

As if to cap off her point, the feedback from Meredith's arguments with the outpost's security appeared at the corner of Nickie's vision. An ever-growing list of blocked fire-suppression attempts as Meredith kept the station's security from running onto the ship and finding a very unwelcome surprise.

Nickie heaved a sigh as if she were being forced to

watch someone eat the last slice of cake she would ever be offered, and she broke into a run toward the docking bay. People stepped aside as she charged along, getting out of the way of both her bull-rush and the look on her face.

Rebus Quadrant Minerva Trading Outpost, Aboard the *Penitent Granddaughter*, Kitchen

It was a simple matter to storm through the corridors to the galley. Nickie was pretty sure the vendor was still shouting on the dock after she sprinted past him and told him to hold his horses. But she hadn't expected to open the door to the galley and find Grim staring at a flaming pot.

He was calm in the way of a man who was standing at the eye of his own storm. At any moment, he might erupt into a panic.

"Aren't you supposed to be a *chef*?" Nickie asked, stepping into the galley and waving smoke out of her face. She could barely even hear herself speaking over the siren and the rioting going on in every direction.

"I don't speak or read Skaine," Grim replied. He very nearly sounded like he was sulking. "I found what looked like red pepper. How was I supposed to know Skaine spices burst into flame?"

Nickie snorted. She couldn't say that was surprising, all things considered, but that wasn't the most helpful observation at that point. "Fire suppression shit?"

Grim seemed half a second away from saying something snide in response before he realized she was probably talking to her EI, who knew where basically everything was.

In the back of the closet on the far wall, Meredith answered promptly.

Nickie scoffed as she jogged over to the closet and started digging through it. Of *course* it was about as far away from the hottest parts of the galley as it could get without being in a different room entirely. That definitely made sense.

She emerged from the closet with a fire-retardant blanket folded in her hands. Grim met her halfway to help unfold it before they tossed it over the pot. It made a steaming, fizzling noise, and a few more gusts of acrid smoke crept out from beneath it.

Abruptly, the siren died down with a final squawk and the lights stopped flashing. It seemed a bit too quick, but Nickie was willing to assume Meredith had shut it down.

Nickie, there's a bit of a situation building next door, Meredith reported, as if the silencing of the fire alarm had simply been her version of clearing her throat.

Nickie groaned and threw her hands up. "What now?"

"Did she mention the noise next door?" Grim asked blandly, lifting the edge of the blanket to peer at the pot underneath. He recoiled when the pot coughed out a puff of semi-noxious gas right in his face.

Of the seven Skaines in the next room, one of them is considerably smaller than average. From what I can interpret, I'm concerned that if someone doesn't let him out of there he's going to be eaten, Meredith supplied.

Nickie blinked slowly. "These guys are cannibals." It was supposed to be a question, but it came out sounding more like a very tired statement. Grim gave her a look like she had just sprouted a few extra heads.

Ordinarily no, Meredith replied, like an eager history teacher. *But it's not entirely unheard of, and a larger one is making threats that seem increasingly likely.*

With a slow sigh that seemed to scream "Why me?" Nickie looked at Grim. "Wait here."

That said, she stepped out of the kitchen again and stopped in front of the door to the next room. *All right, let's get this over with.*

Meredith opened the door so abruptly that the three Skaines clustered in front of it toppled into the hall. One by one, Nickie booted them back into the room and stepped inside. The door closed once again, sealing her in but making it so none of the Skaine could make a run for it while she was occupied.

The largest of them didn't even come up to Nickie's nose, but he was nearly twice as broad as she was. He was standing in front of a pair of cabinets, and it took Nickie a moment to realize that a considerably smaller Skaine was huddled on the floor between the cabinets.

Nickie arched one eyebrow pointedly. "Really?" She sighed like a disappointed parent. "Twelve hours without food and you jump straight to cannibalism? Most people would go for, like, their boots or their belts before going straight for their coworkers."

"Uh, Krask?" one of the average sized Skaines asked. "What do we do about her?"

The larger one—Krask, presumably—heaved a sigh and turned to face Nickie, ignoring the cabinets and the runt for the time being. "You get out of the way and let me handle this."

Like a sea parting, five of the Skaines huddled back

against the walls, getting well out of the way as Krask charged. Nickie sidestepped, stuck a leg out, and sent Krask tumbling to the floor when he tripped over it. She knew her enhancements were just waiting there for her to use them, but she got the impression she wasn't going to need them for this.

Krask caught his balance against the wall and whirled toward Nickie again in a hail of flying fists. She blocked one strike, then the next, and wove away from the next two. Finally, she clamped her hands around the sides of Krask's head, forcing him to come to a halt if he didn't want to wind up snapping his own neck.

Nickie's grip tightened, and she slammed one knee straight into Krask's chest. She let him go, and he sank to the floor in a wheezing heap. Around them, five of the Skaines muttered to each other uncomfortably and shifted closer to the walls. They had no interest in getting their asses handed to them.

"Don't just stand there!" Krask wheezed as he caught his breath. "Do something! You saw what just happened!"

The others hesitated for a moment—if the strongest of them had landed on his ass, they didn't have much hope for themselves—before they decided that Krask was scarier than the challenge ahead of them. As one they lunged at Nickie, hoping numbers would give them an edge.

Nickie pirouetted out of the way, so two of them slammed into each other and tumbled to the floor in a heap of tangled limbs. As they disentangled themselves, Nickie caught the arm of a third Skaine trying to rush her. Grip tight, she ducked an incoming blow from a fourth and turned in a swift circle, letting go at the last minute so that the Skaine in her grasp crashed into the wall like a crash-test dummy.

She slammed one elbow into the side of another Skaine's head, and he dropped to the floor on top of the two who were still trying to regain their footing. Already, there were four out of the way, and she turned her gaze to the fifth.

The clever one of the bunch, apparently. He looked back and forth between the Skaines on the floor and Nickie before he held his hands up in surrender and sat down right there on the floor. Nickie offered him a toothy shark-like grin and nodded once. There was no time to celebrate just then, though. She wasn't quite finished.

Krask got back to his feet just in time for Nickie to kick out with one leg, catching him in the chin with the heel of her boot. His head snapped back, and he toppled to the floor once again.

Nickie stood in the middle of the room for a moment to make sure nothing else was going to happen. Once she was certain that she was in the clear, she walked toward the back of the room. She stopped in front of the cabinets the runt was still hiding between and offered him a hand. "Come with me if you want to live."

Really? Meredith sighed.

The runt wasted no time in taking her hand and letting Nickie pull him to his feet and lead him out of the room. They stepped through the door quickly once it opened, and it locked behind them once again as soon as they were through.

Grim poked his head out of the galley, offering a sullen, "You're all so loud." He was fanning smoke toward one of the ventilation ducts with a hand towel, the filtration system working overtime.

Nickie rolled her eyes, but before she could complain Grim sighed and offered, "I'll keep an eye on him while you finish whatever you were doing. He can help me clean up this mess."

With a distracted nod Nickie ushered the Skaine into the galley with Grim, and as she turned to head back to the airlock, she just barely caught him offering his name. She made a note of it. She would probably have to remember it later.

In the meantime, there was a very angry merchant still waiting in the docking bay for her to make the second half of her payment and collect her delivery.

Twenty minutes later, she was unboxing supplies as she sat on the floor in a storage closet. Her bank account was considerably less robust than it had been that morning.

Let's get out of here, she decided as she tore a box open, though she made no move to get up.

I'm on it, Meredith assured her, and she set about bypassing the various pre-flight checks. The docking tube disengaged, along with the locks that held the ship in place. The floor hummed as the engine engaged, and within just a few minutes the ship was pulling out of the dock.

Rebus Quadrant, Aboard the *Penitent Granddaughter*

Nickie stretched, sitting back and arching her spine until it popped. She was still sitting on the floor in the closet and it looked as if she were sitting in a nest, considering the empty, torn-apart packaging surrounding her.

In front of her sat four little house bots. Fully assembled but not yet activated, each was a different metallic color. They were neatly bullet-shaped, with several little arms recessed within their plating and an array of circular sensors around their tops and bottoms that looked like eyes.

They were almost absurdly adorable, which made perfect sense for commercial bots designed for household use. They didn't come any higher than Nickie's knees in their powered-off state, and already she couldn't help but think they looked like they were napping.

She really needed a few other people on the ship. She was personifying the vacuum cleaners.

Her ship was probably a little bigger than what they were designed for, but that was why there were four of them. They could help each other.

With a slow sigh, Nickie patted one of them on its rounded top. *What do you think, Meredith? Could we link them with your systems?*

It would be helpful to give them the schematics to the ship, Meredith acknowledged. *Otherwise, you would have to hunt down the blueprints and upload them manually.*

Plus then you'll have your own army of tiny robots, Nickie replied, grinning. *You could sic them on anyone who tried to board the ship without permission.*

I'm not sure what a quartet of cleaner bots could do against an invading force, but I suppose you're not wrong, Meredith acknowledged dryly.

Nickie scoffed. *You just need to have a sense of imagination about it, is all,* she assured the EI, sitting back and leaning her weight on her hands. *Let's get these little guys started up.*

It's a mess in here, so this should be as good a trial run for them as anything.

You certainly didn't make any efforts to be neat about unboxing them, Meredith remarked, but she did as she was requested regardless. She dug through the ship's storage banks until she found the ship's blueprints.

Once one of them is properly set up it should communicate with the others, but for me to set it up you will need to turn one of them on, Meredith pointed out. *I can't use the wireless network if it's inactive.*

Nickie flashed a thumbs-up to thin air and picked up the bot she had most recently assembled, still sitting in a clear space of the floor between her knees. She turned it this way and that, flipping it upside down and peering at it from every angle as she looked for an On switch.

"I can do it," she snapped aloud before Meredith even had a chance to offer any advice.

She set it back down on the floor, squinted at it, and took note of how its rounded head was slightly raised above the rest of it. She curled one hand over the top of it and pressed down. The head lowered a few millimeters before popping back to its usual spot.

It hummed quietly and played a merry little jingle as its sensors lit up, then rose a few centimeters off its base and spun in a cheery circle. It turned until the screen on its front was facing Nickie.

Hello! Thank you for waking me up! Please select a network!

Nickie tugged it closer and tapped the buttons on the screen until it connected to the ship's primary wireless network.

All yours, Nickie announced, leaning back on her hands again. Out of the corner of her eye, she watched the progress of Meredith's work scroll past, until the little bot dinged like a caffeinated microwave when the upload of the blueprint finished. Immediately, the bot's various arms popped out of their casings as it started picking up the scattered pieces of trash. It trundled off in the direction of the nearest trash chute once its arms were full, and Nickie turned her attention to the other three bots. One by one she activated them and connected them to the network, but she left it up to the first bot to fill them in on what they were supposed to be doing.

Soon enough, the three newly-activated bots were laden with trash and on their way to the chute, following the first one.

Still sitting on the floor, Nickie watched them bustle away. She waited until the closet door slid closed again before she said to no one in particular, "Wow. Those are fucking adorable."

Back in her quarters, she found she had time before she had to get involved with serving Grim's cuisine to the Skaine prisoners.

Just enough time to relax and find out what pearls of wisdom Aunt Tabitha has in store for me, she thought to herself, slouching back onto the bed with her boots still on.

She pulled up the file and began reading again.

CHAPTER 7 TABITHA

Farha Station

Hirotoshi and Tabitha were arguing good-naturedly when the other Tontos descended the gangway of the small ship.

They had made the decision not to take *Achronyx*, thinking that their usual ship might be on the radar of Skaines everywhere. Where possible, they wanted to take enemies by surprise, and traveling on the *Achronyx* was like carrying a flashing neon sign: *I'm Tabitha, and I'm here to fuck you up. Start running.*

Tabitha's eyes narrowed. She couldn't decide if she wanted to give them enough warning to start running, or just drop in on them and kill them.

Probably the second. There were a lot of Skaines, and even though she would have a long life, it was going to take a while to kill them all.

She looked over when the other Tontos joined them.

"Hirotoshi and I are going to find a bar." She considered. "Ryu, you come with us."

After all, while Hirotoshi was always dull—or so she said, mainly just to annoy him—Ryu could sometimes be persuaded to have some fun with her.

The others exchanged glances, promising a future conversation, but they made sure that Tabitha and Hirotoshi didn't see it.

"We will stay on the ship in case of, umm…" Katsu considered how to put this tactfully, and gave Jun and Kouki a look. "In case we need to leave very quickly?" he suggested finally.

"Or in case we need backup," Tabitha added. She gave a self-satisfied smile. "After all, we don't want anyone to know *all* our numbers up front."

"Kemosabe—" Hirotoshi began.

"*Nope.* We're doing this. Come on, Ryu." Tabitha waved to the others and led Hirotoshi and Ryu across the landing bay toward the main part of Farha station.

The three watched them go.

"They are going to get in a fight," Katsu predicted. "Do we take an over-under on how long it will take?"

"I have a better idea," Jun suggested. "We take a bet on which will get into a fight *first*. I will bet on Tabitha."

"That's not fair," Kouki argued. "*Everyone* would bet on Tabitha."

"I will take Ryu," Katsu countered. "It is highly likely that someone in a seedy bar will say something to provoke him."

"That leaves me with Hirotoshi," Kouki complained.

"You should have spoken up faster," Jun told him solemnly. "Fortune favors the quick."

Kouki just shook his head. "What does the winner get?"

"Haven't you been paying attention?" Katsu asked him. "It isn't the winner. It's the loser. The loser *gets* to do a lot of push-ups. I think, in this case, perhaps...five hundred?"

The other two considered and then nodded.

"That is a good number," Jun agreed.

"It will take forever," Kouki added. "But at least we won't have Bethany Anne standing on our backs—in heels."

"Yes." Katsu stared toward where the others had disappeared. "Tabitha is a merciful leader that way. Let's go back to the ship before people notice us and carry word to whoever is in those bars. And let's keep the ship warmed up anyway. Without Achronyx here to run everything, I want to make *sure* we can get away quickly if we need to."

Jun waved to where the three of them had disappeared. "Tabitha can deal with whatever fights they get into," he argued as he followed Katsu up the gangway.

"Normally, I would agree with you," Katsu replied, "but recently Kemosabe has not been very discerning. Right now she is motivated more by revenge than Justice."

"I worry," Kouki chimed in. He looked at the docking bay. "I wish we could help her."

"We *are* helping her," Katsu replied. "There is nothing that will take her grief away. It must be felt, lived, and survived. We are here with her while she grieves, just as she is with us while we grieve."

The three were silent as they made their way to the bridge. Though they had made it a point not to show their grief openly, that did not mean they were not grieving.

Shin's loss had hit them all deeply.

Despite their centuries and the friends they had lost over the years, the Tontos felt each death keenly.

Katsu wondered if Shin's death had hit them harder because he was the first to be lost away from Earth. He could not be buried at any of the locations in Japan he had liked best.

His ashes would not return to the dust of his home planet.

In some ways, Shin's death had made it clearer than anything else that they were *never* returning to their home.

Katsu shook his head slightly and took a seat in the captain's chair.

Shin had been given a chance at redemption and had died a good death, serving honorable ends. No one could ask for more. Katsu refused to mourn as though the worst had occurred.

If he had been younger, however...yes. He would be angry at the whole universe for Shin's death.

Meanwhile, Tabitha was striding through the space station with her long coat swinging behind her. She kept her arms loose, ready to grab her Jean Dukes if she needed them, and the look on her face told the aliens around her to just *try* pulling something.

She hoped they did.

Anything to distract her from the aching void that never seemed far from swallowing her. The others had tried to be there for her, but all of them were so restrained in their grief and so elegant in their responses that she was embarrassed to tell them how she felt.

She was sure Hirotoshi had never cried until he was

covered in snot. Tabitha's lip crinkled up in the corner just a tiny bit. *That was fucking funny!*

She had spent a lot of nights in her room sobbing into a pillow and punching things, and then she had realized that not only was it not bringing Shin back, none of it was helping to avenge him.

That was why she was here. The Skaines didn't care who they hurt or killed. She'd already been determined to stop them, and now...

Her gloves were off.

They found a bar pretty quickly. Barnabas was fond of saying that it was the one constant all over the universe: no matter where you were, there was always somewhere to get a drink. Tabitha had used that wisdom more often than she expected.

Now she would use it to hunt snitches.

They swept through the doors, and Tabitha decided to go to the bar first. Some places got picky if you just took a table.

She flashed a bit of money, cash picked up in her travels. She didn't want to just blow in somewhere and show a bunch of Etheric Empire coins. That wasn't the sort of attention she wanted...yet.

"Hi," she said to the bartender. It was tall and slender, whatever kind of alien it was, and its blue head bent curiously toward her. "Drinks for my two friends and me?"

"Of course." Its voice echoed vaguely. "You understand, kind patron, that no guarantees are made regarding our drinks' toxicity and your physiology?"

"Yes, yes, "Tabitha agreed, tapping the coins on the bar. "What would you recommend?"

"Ah. For legal reasons, kind patron—"

"I get it." Tabitha rolled her eyes. "You can't recommend anything because it all might be toxic. You know, most places would just recommend the most expensive thing on the menu and be done with it."

"Kind patron, I assure you that your friend would never attempt to cheat you."

"An honest salesman?" Tabitha damn near wanted to roll her eyes. *Was the universe just fucking with her?* She looked at Hirotoshi and Ryu. "What are the odds?"

"Very slim, Kemosabe." Hirotoshi's face was his trademark deadpan. "One might call it miraculous."

Tabitha looked around the bar until she saw someone with vaguely similar coloring to a human's. She had learned over her travels that people who were colored like humans tended to have the physical properties and resistances.

It wasn't perfect, but it was the best indicator so far.

"Three of what he's having." She nodded her head at the patron.

"At once, kind patron. That will be...what currency are you using? Ah, yes—716 edru."

"Here." Tabitha slid the cash across the counter. She had no idea what sort of cash was generally used in this system, but edru were weighted metal, easily verified, and so were easy to acquire and get rid of again.

"Where should we sit?" Hirotoshi asked as the bartender gave them their drinks.

The alien waved at the tables. "Anywhere you wish, kind patron."

"Thank you." Hirotoshi led the way purposefully

through the bar. "If I had to hear it say 'kind patron' once more, I was going to do it violence."

Tabitha exchanged a grin with Ryu. Hirotoshi liked to pretend he didn't have any sort of temper, but they had seen it enough to be amused when it came out.

Tabitha took care to make herself visible. She knew all eyes were on them as the strange new aliens in this sector, but she wanted to make doubly sure that people saw her. She let the coat swing open at times so people could see flashes of the Jean Dukes, and she moved with the same predatory grace as Ryu and Hirotoshi.

"Now what, Kemosabe?" Ryu asked when they were seated. "How does one—how did you put it?—hunt snitches?"

Hirotoshi gave a sniff and looked off in the distance as he sipped his drink. His nose wrinkled slightly. "This is wretched."

"How could you possibly besmirch *this*?" Tabitha lifted her glass. "This is a specialty of Farha Station, and I will have you know—" She cut off her diatribe by taking a large swallow…and her face scrunched before she spat it all over the table. She reached for a cloth to toss on the mess as she looked at what was left in her glass. "Oh, my God, that's the worst. That's so bad. Sonofa…" She brought it up to her nose. "Is this donkey piss?"

Hirotoshi, who hadn't touched his drink, calmly answered, "I don't think they have donkeys out here."

"Oh, God, it could be anything." Tabitha was wiping her tongue on her palm.

He shook his head and sighed. "Kemosabe, I assure you that your nanites will—"

"No, it's that I have to live, knowing I've drunk this. The memory is too much." She gave a full body shudder. "Urgh. Hurk. *Yech*." She eyed the cloth, wondering if she had cooties from touching it.

Hirotoshi shook his head, and a tall alien staggered over him and shoved him to the floor. There was a blare of alien language, too quick for their implants to interpret.

"What did he say?" Ryu asked Tabitha in an undertone.

Tabitha played back the audio with the translation. "He says...he doesn't like Hirotoshi's face."

Ryu turned to his friend. "Well, who does, really?" he asked whimsically.

Hirotoshi stood. He didn't look as upset as Ryu knew him to be. His chest was rising and falling a bit more emphatically, and the two of them could see the tension around his nose.

Which for Hirotoshi, meant he looked furious, but he nodded stiffly to the alien and sat down once again.

"He did that on purpose." Hirotoshi shrugged.

The alien pushed Hirotoshi's shoulder, and this time everyone's implants caught what he said.

"Your face offends me," he argued again.

Tabitha looked at them. "Seriously, is this a scene from Star Wars?"

Ryu snapped his fingers. "I *thought* I'd seen this before."

Hirotoshi's long-suffering gaze rolled across the two of them.

Hirotoshi stood up and looked at the alien.

Tabitha nodded. "Notice how he hasn't spilled his drink yet?"

Ryu looked at his glass, his lips pressed together. "That

should be rectified, shortly if he doesn't want to find a new reason to wish for death."

Hirotoshi, one eyebrow raised, placed the glass on the table. He adjusted his cuffs and coat slightly and stared the alien down.

"I did not mean to upset you," he replied. "I *apologize*, and hope you will forgive me for any offense."

"That man has the patience of a saint," Ryu muttered to Tabitha under his breath. "It does *not* make for good television."

Tabitha snickered, but they stopped hastily when Hirotoshi turned to look at them as if to say, "You could help me instead of laughing, you know."

"Hey." Tabitha stood up and walked around the table to sling an arm around the alien's shoulders. She waved a casual finger in Hirotoshi's direction. "What don't you like about him?"

"It looked at me funny," the alien growled. It curled its lip at Hirotoshi. "Look at his face. It's an affront."

Tabitha looked at Ryu, who shrugged. In the beginning, she hadn't been able to tell the vampires apart, so she had no idea why this alien didn't like Hirotoshi in particular.

"Kemosabe," Hirotoshi disgustedly told Tabitha in Japanese, "please explain to our friend that I mean no offense and am only trying to enjoy my drink."

"Good luck with that," Ryu muttered.

"I *could* do that," Tabitha replied in the same language, "but it wouldn't be as much fun." She turned to the alien. "I know this man. He picks fights wherever he goes."

Hirotoshi's face went completely blank. "*Kemosabe!*"

"He wants to pick a fight with me?" The alien shook her arm off. "I won't bother with him, then."

"Wait, what?" Tabitha shook her head. "That's not right."

Hirotoshi shot Tabitha a serenely satisfied look.

She shook her head. "No, what he *needs* is for someone to knock his face in," Tabitha urged. "Most people can't do it, but I bet you could."

Hirotoshi's face turned stony as the alien eyed him. "Most people can't fight him?" He pointed at Hirotoshi but looked at Tabitha with what could best be described as amusement. "*Him?*"

Tabitha nodded. "Sure, he doesn't look like much, I'll give you that." Her eyes were dancing. "But he *can* fight. I mean, pretty well I'm led to believe."

Hirotoshi told Tabitha, "Our next practice session, I will show *you* pretty well—"

The alien launched himself at Hirotoshi with a roar, and Tabitha stepped neatly out of the way. In her earpiece, she could hear Katsu asking if it was Hirotoshi who'd gotten in a fight first.

She winced as the alien tried to slam a chair over Hirotoshi, who sidestepped it. "It was strange, like he was trying to be an ass. He kept prodding the alien, and it was all I could do to—"

"I won!" Katsu yelled after being informed by Ryu that it was.

"Like hell, someone's betting and I'm not involved!" Tabitha shot back. "New bet, Ryu, Hirotoshi. Whoever punches the most people wins!"

She didn't wait to see what the others thought of her

bet before leaping into action. One of the alien's friends was coming at Hirotoshi with both hands up. Tabitha wasn't sure what his plan was, but this was a brawl. Brawls had one rule: beat everyone up except your friends.

Other than the rule that there were bars in every location, this was the second most universal rule. It probably had something to do with the fact that so many of the fights were due to alcohol or its equivalents, and those were served in bars.

Which were in every system already. In this case, she figured correlation was causation.

Tabitha picked the alien up and heaved him over her shoulder. He caught a table on the way down, and there was the clatter of silverware and shattering glass.

"Music to my ears." Tabitha grinned when another alien slammed sideways into her. "*Sonofabitch!*" She collided with a table violently and skidded, the alien's full weight driving her into the metal edge. "Fuck, you're heavy. What do you eat for breakfast, fucking cannonballs?"

"That seems unlikely, Kemosabe." Hirotoshi had maddeningly regained his composure, she noticed. He was brawling with enough efficiency and grace that it appeared to be show-fighting, not a proper brawl.

"Loosen up a bit, Hirotoshi!" Tabitha yelled back at him. She slammed her elbow sideways into the chest region of the alien who had tackled her and grunted in satisfaction when it gave a bellow of pain. "Gotcha, you big blue bastard!"

"I don't know what your count is," Ryu called, "but I am up to six." He leapt nimbly onto one of the tables to avoid a tackle, then jumped down once more onto his opponent, driving a fist down as he did so. "Seven," he amended.

"I am falling behind." Tabitha punched the blue alien three times before he had time to put up his guard.

"That counts as one, Kemosabe," Hirotoshi told her gravely. He spun in a circle, fists lashing. "I am now up to eight. Also, both of you be careful not to spill my drink."

"Why the hell would you *want* to drink that?" Tabitha yelled back. "I should do you a favor and spill it!"

"I wish to appreciate the fine culture of Farha Station." Hirotoshi lashed out with his leg and caught an opponent in the temple with his heel. "I should have asked. Do kicks count?"

"*No*," Tabitha and Ryu chorused together. As usual, Hirotoshi was up on the two of them when it came to fights.

Three aliens rushed Tabitha at once. She leapt into the air and scissored her legs out, catching two of them in the face, then came down and flipped the other onto a nearby table. She dragged him back off and punched him in the face.

He went down like a stone.

The other two got up dazedly, and a flurry of punches directed at each managed to take them down again. Tabitha couldn't be sure exactly *which* part of their anatomy to hit to take them out of the fight, so she needed to hit them in many places very quickly.

Luckily for her, punching was a form of exercise, and she had been told to keep up her exercising.

Many of the remaining patrons fled into the main part

of the station, screaming, but one of the remaining aliens was rushing toward the humans…

And the table with Hirotoshi's beverage.

"Dammit. Hirotoshi!" Tabitha grabbed the alien and swung him, but he was much heavier than he appeared. "Oh shit!"

Hirotoshi plucked the drink off the table as Tabitha arced through the air and smashed onto it, taking the tabletop to the floor.

"I believe you're losing," he remarked, taking a sip of his drink. "What did we say the forfeit was?"

Tabitha's eyes flashed red as she climbed to her feet. "Losing? Oh, it is *on*. Get ready, Donkey Kong!"

CHAPTER 8 TABITHA

Farha Station

It had been a terrible day, but Edif was finally relaxing with a beer. He'd been minding his own business when the fight broke out.

He didn't look up. It was just Okk, one of the station's more notorious bastards.

Okk had never met a newcomer he didn't want to punch, and apparently, no force in the universe could stop him from doing it, so most everyone had given up at this point.

Okk would run off the newcomers, and everything would go back to being quiet.

Then Guildert, a local Torcellan information broker, landed on Edif's table and broke it. A few seconds later Okk followed, and then a brawl broke out like Edif had not yet seen.

And, well, it *had* been a bad day.

He drained his drink, uttered an old battle cry his

grandfather had taught him, and charged at one of the newcomers. If it was going to be a fight, he was going to get in on it, dammit!

He decided to work his way up by going for the smallest one. The short, pale alien with dark hair on its head was wearing a long coat and carrying two absurdly large pistols. Retrospectively he would decide he should have paid attention to how large those guns were, but at the time he didn't hesitate.

The alien was talking with one of its compatriots when Edif charged. He managed to take it over sideways and directed a punch at its head.

"It's been a bad day, alien." He bared his teeth at it. It had flat teeth, which would make it a stupid herbivore, right? "And you're about to suffer for it. But, hell, you got into this fight, didn't you?"

Its eyes flashed red, and it bared its teeth as it cocked its head to the side. "I don't think *I'm* going to suffer," it said.

And its teeth started to lengthen.

Edif shoved himself back with a scream. "Demon! Demon!"

Tabitha laughed hysterically as she picked him up, whipped him around her head, and slammed him back to the floor.

"It's been a bad day, alien," she mocked him. "And *you're* about to suffer for it. But, hell, you got into this fight, didn't you?"

Nearby, Hirotoshi gave a small shake of his head as he drove an elbow into another alien's face. The thing howled and spurted purplish blood, which he stepped out of the way of.

This new ship didn't wash his shirts very well.

He slammed his fist into another alien as the thing charged him, and tackled two more as they went for Ryu's back.

Tabitha was still taunting the one, trading punches with it and not getting any closer to winning the bet.

Her loss.

Hirotoshi and Ryu faced each other as they each dispatched their latest enemies.

"Eleven," Hirotoshi asserted.

"Eleven," Ryu echoed dangerously.

They looked around to where the last alien in the bar was looking at them with a sort of panicked expression, and both of them took off like a shot.

The alien fled, screaming, but it wasn't fast enough. Hirotoshi reached it by a slim margin—possibly aided, though he would never admit it, by the fact that Ryu had *somehow* been shoved sideways into a puddle of spilled liquor—and his punch sent the alien skidding across the lobby outside to sprawl in a sad-looking stand of fake potted plants.

"And I win," Hirotoshi murmured, bowing.

"I want a rematch." Ryu's face, as he wiped liquor off of his hand, was annoyed.

Meanwhile, Tabitha had released her opponent, who stumbled away with a little moan was looking around.

"Dammit." She went up to the bar, where the bartender was polishing glasses as if nothing noteworthy had happened. "A glass of something *different* than you gave me last time, and the names of three snitches, please."

"What is a snitch?" the bartender inquired. He placed a

glass on the bar and filled it. "Here you go, kind patron. You will be pleased to know that according to bar rules, all subsequent drinks are bought by the person who begins a bar fight. That would be Okk."

Tabitha looked around. "Okk?" A muffled whimper of pain sounded from somewhere amidst the broken furniture and Tabitha hoisted her glass in a toast. "Thanks for the drink, man."

She turned back to the bartender and took a sip. Her eyebrows went up as she drained it and then looked at the empty glass.

"Damn, this is *good*."

The bartender nodded. "I am gratified to hear it, kind patron."

"Hirotoshi's right. You need to stop saying that." She patted the bar. "But regarding snitches. Let's say information brokers. Where would I find one of those?"

"Ah." The bartended only barely kept himself from referring to her as "kind patron" again. "You would want to speak to Guildert. He is a Torcellan."

"Where would I find him?"

The bartender gestured with one towel-bearing hand toward a particularly large pile of unconscious brawlers. "Under that pile of bodies."

"Well, fuck." Tabitha grimaced. "That isn't how I like to begin business relationships. At least it will show him I'm serious, though, right?" She waved a hand in a circle. "Yo, Tontos." She pointed. "We need to find a Torcellan in that pile."

Ryu and Hirotoshi walked over curiously, and for a few moments the only sounds in the bar were the thuds and whimpers of unconscious people being picked up, examined, and dropped to the side, and the *clunks* of clean glasses being set on the bar by the bartender.

Finally, they reached a pale figure with lights still twinkling in his hair. Tabitha pointed at him curiously.

"That Guildert?" she asked. He nodded.

"Okay, one more question. Where's the nearest seedy hotel?"

"Upstairs." The bartender smiled. "Five hundred edru and no questions asked."

"Well, then." Tabitha put the money on the counter and nodded to Ryu, who picked up the Torcellan and slung him over his shoulder.

They headed upstairs and made their way down a dingy, sticky hallway to an equally dingy and sticky room, where Tabitha tied the Torcellan to the foot of the bed and Hirotoshi pulled a syringe out of a hidden protective pocket in his coat.

Ryu and Tabitha frowned at him, and he smiled. "It's a secret." Then he reached down and slapped the Torcellan in the face. "You. Wake up."

"What..." Guildert shook his head from side to side, looking around. "Where am I?"

"Not important." Tabitha considered. "Let's just say, no one's going to come looking for you here. Now that that's out of the way—"

"Why are you holding me captive?" He yanked at the handcuffs, looking panicked.

"Because I've never met a trustworthy information broker, that's why." Tabitha crouched near him. "So here's the deal. You're going to give me information on the

Skaines. Where I can find them. Where any big slaving or drug running operations are going down. Then I'm going to pay you because I am not a thief, but I am going to pay you a reasonable amount and not whatever trumped-up price you give outsiders because you're tied to a bed and I'm not an idiot." She patted his face. "Sound good?"

The Torcellan pushed with his legs and tried to draw himself up. "I do *not* make deals without establishing the price of the information, and without being free to choose or decline the contract."

"Ohhhh." Tabitha nodded. "So you're saying you can't deal with us while you're all tied up?"

"Precisely." The Torcellan inclined his head.

Tabitha pursed her lips, then shrugged. "Ok, sure, I get it." She stepped back and gestured at the Torcellan. "Hirotoshi, shoot him."

"Wait, wait!" The Torcellan flailed wildly, jerking at his bonds. "Don't kill me! For the love of all gods, don't kill me! I'll tell you what you want to know!"

"You know, this really was an unnecessary diversion," Tabitha commented.

"It was," Hirotoshi agreed. He looked into the Torcellan's eyes and allowed his teeth to lengthen somewhat. "Shall we agree not to have any such diversions from here on out?"

"Yes, yes." The Torcellan nodded so fast his head hit the bottom of the bed a few times, then winced as the pain shot through him. "Of course. No diversions."

"Excellent." Tabitha sat in one of the chairs and gave a pained look. "It's *sticky*."

"I suggest you throw those pants out when you get back

to the ship," Ryu commented. "Don't even try washing them. You realize you're probably sitting in a pile of alien—"

"Eewwwww!" Tabitha stood up, pushed the chair at the wall, and shuddered when it hit the floor in pieces. "Oh, God. This day has been disgusting. Hirotoshi, get the information we want. I've still got the heebie-jeebies crawling all over this body, and this body is supposed to *give* heebie-jeebies, not get them."

"Mmm," Hirotoshi murmured. He looked at the Torcellan again. "You were going to tell us about the Skaines?"

"There is a deal happening nearby." The Torcellan swallowed as he stared into those red eyes. "I-I helped set it up. They're trading guns for...for slaves. And drugs."

"Ah." Tabitha's face went stony. "You helped set it up?"

"I..." The Torcellan looked like he was going to faint.

"I don't suppose we have time for recreational torture," Tabitha suggested. "Just a few electrodes, maybe?"

"If you leave now, you can still make the rendezvous!" the Torcellan gasped. "It is happening in no more than half a day. It is in the Dwest system, the one with the binary stars, one red and one blue. If you go now... If you go *now*—"

"If we don't take the time to torture you, you mean?"

The Torcellan shook his head but said, "Yes!"

"Hmmm." Tabitha looked at Ryu and Hirotoshi and asked over the comm, "Katsu, what do you think? Jun? Kouki?"

Katsu's voice came back sounding very pleased. "Jun and Kouki are doing push-ups, so I'll vote for all of us. We know where this slimeball is, so why don't we go for the deal and come back for him later?"

Ryu and Hirotoshi nodded slightly to indicate their agreement and Tabitha shrugged.

"Looks like it's your lucky day, buddy boy. Give us the details."

The Torcellan gasped them out. The meeting would take place on one of the continents on the planet below, an island about half the size of Australia. There, in the shadow of an erupting volcano, there would be so much radio interference that no one would notice the deal going down unless they flew directly overhead…which, of course, no one was going to do with the volcano there.

Tabitha relayed the information to Katsu. "Can you verify any of this?" she subvocalized.

"One moment," he replied. The three stared at the Torcellan, who was sweating. Katsu's voice came back. "The facts he's giving seem to be correct regarding the eruption and the island. Moreover, two Skaine warships left this station yesterday, heading in the vague direction of that rendezvous point. We should be able to easily make it there in time."

Tabitha looked around. "Damn. I was kind of hoping to be able to kill him. That fight really didn't take the edge off." The Torcellan's eyes opened a bit wider.

"Soon you will have many Skaines to kill," Katsu pointed out.

She smiled. "You always know what to say."

Tabitha nodded to Ryu and Hirotoshi. "Let's go." To the spluttering Torcellan, she added, "We'll make sure someone gets the message to come get you tomorrow." She swept out, adding under her breath, "But *we'll* be back for you soon, asswipe."

Ryu followed her, but Hirotoshi knelt beside the Torcellan and pushed his sleeve up. The needle pierced the skin, and the Torcellan drew his breath in sharply as Hirotoshi dispensed the liquid into his bloodstream.

"Have you ever met a smart virus before?" Hirotoshi asked.

The Torcellan shook his head, looking terrified.

"This will activate in thirty-six hours unless we come back to the station and give you the antidote," Hirotoshi explained.

He noticed Ryu and Tabitha peering back at him. "So if you did not give us the correct information and we are walking into a trap, now would be the time to tell us. Otherwise, you will die when we do not return."

"It was correct!" the Torcellan blubbered, looking from Hirotoshi to Ryu to Tabitha, then at his arm. "It was, I swear! No trap! I spoke honestly!"

"Good." Hirotoshi smiled. "That's good. We'll see you soon, then." He stood, pocketed the syringe, and left with Ryu and Tabitha.

They made it to the main plaza before Ryu broke.

"Where did you get a smart virus? I didn't know that was a—"

"It was vitamin B," Hirotoshi explained. He gave a sharp smile. "It does absolutely nothing to Torcellans—or most other species, for that matter. I carry it purely for persuasive reasons."

Ryu and Tabitha exchanged shocked glances before they both started laughing.

"He's a stone-cold bastard," Tabitha remarked in appreciation.

"He makes good use of technology," Ryu agreed. "It's one of the good things about him. Always willing to adapt to his circumstances."

Hirotoshi only looked forward.

They returned to the ship to find Jun and Kouki just finishing up their push-ups. Jun gave Tabitha an annoyed look.

"You disappointed me. I bet on *you* to get into a fight first."

"I won," Katsu gloated, with a smooth smile. He nodded to Hirotoshi. "My compliments on your successful brawl."

Hirotoshi tried to look disapproving, but his lips were twitching when he went to the bridge to lay in coordinates.

The journey, such as it was, was quick, although there was time for Tabitha to throw her pants in the wash and then decide to throw them out anyway, while the team pored over the extra information the Torcellan had provided.

He must have had a voice-activated communication device. There were a few leads and some assorted tidbits about the captains of the two Skaine ships that had previously docked at Farha Station.

"He's really trying to get on our good side, huh?" Jun asked. He was adjusting his armor. They had set down near the volcano, cloaked, and were just waiting for Tabitha to finish showering.

"He is." Hirotoshi surveyed one of the recent messages. "But I really don't care about the captain's sexual habits. We don't want to blackmail him, we want to kill him."

"You never know when it could be useful," Kouki countered.

"When what could be useful?" Tabitha came into the conference room, her hair still drying from her third shower. She caught sight of the message, and her eyes went wide. "That's not what I think it is, right? Oh, my God, it's even worse. How does that fit *there*? No, don't tell me. I don't want to know."

"Mmm." Hirotoshi nodded at her and brought up the screen. "As you see, the two ships are present, and a third appears to be very close. We stand ready to move, but there is a complication."

"Three ships full of Skaines with slaves in the middle of everything is more than we should try to handle on our own," Ryu explained, taking up the narrative. "We have no idea what self-destruct devices they might have, and what weaponry their ships have."

"What would you like to do, Kemosabe?" Hirotoshi asked. A moment later, he turned to look at her. "Kemosabe?"

But Tabitha was no longer in the room, and a moment later, an automated alert told them that Tabitha had opened the main hatch of the ship.

Hirotoshi switched on his comm, his face taut with worry. "Tabitha—"

"I am going to kill every one of them," Tabitha told them, her voice shaking, "with my bare hands if I have to."

CHAPTER 9 TABITHA

Farha Station

"You were supposed to be watching her!" Hirotoshi hissed at Ryu.

"Me?" Ryu rolled his eyes. "*You're* Number One. *You* were supposed to be watching her!"

"I don't want to interrupt," Jun interjected calmly from the edge of the room, a finger pointing to the screen. "But she has somehow managed to lock us all in here."

Ryu and Hirotoshi looked around at once, and Ryu swore under his breath.

"How the hell did she do that?" Hirotoshi strode to the door and banged on it. "Maybe she's still on the ship."

"No, I'm not," Tabitha's voice came back. "You all stay there. I am going to fuck some Skaines *up*."

"Kemosabe, there are three ships full of Skaines." Hirotoshi was struggling to keep his voice level. "Let us help."

Tabitha considered for a moment. "Nope," she replied finally. "I'll be back in a bit. Stay there."

"Like hell," Ryu muttered. He beckoned Katsu to the door and stood aside as the vampire began tapping the keypad, trying to hack their way out of the room.

Since Tabitha was apparently listening, they decided to mime the rest of their plans. Jun made gestures to show that he would stay with the ship and come rescue them if they needed it.

Hirotoshi gestured to himself, Kouki, and Ryu to say that they would go fight with Tabitha, and Katsu tapped himself on the chest to say that he would go too. Hirotoshi shook his head, and Katsu made a series of gestures that seemed to indicate the three warships.

Hirotoshi threw his hands up, seeming to accede. Kouki just watched.

Ryu, meanwhile, appeared to have started a game of charades with Jun.

At the keypad, Katsu kept tapping away. He was close to undoing what Tabitha had done, but the problem was that she always seemed to come at her programming a bit side-ways—and with a mischievous sense of humor—and he couldn't be sure he wasn't just coding his way into a trap.

Outside the ship, Tabitha made her way across the ground with a few looks up at the volcano. So far it was only spewing billowing clouds of smoke, but who knew when that might change?

She'd give a *lot* to see a big chunk of flaming rock take out a Skaine slaver. *Splat!* She grinned to herself as she made her way through the greenery.

She was careful not to touch any of the plants if she could avoid it. They looked a lot like various tropical plants on Earth, some with broad and vibrantly-colored leaves, others with rough bark, and she had learned the hard way during her travels that pretty things could be very, very dangerous.

Why, just a few weeks ago, some poor petty officer on a routine mission had decided to touch what looked like a nice, soft plant leaf.

He'd wound up in the medical bay, hacking purple stuff out of his lungs until the Pod-doc had managed to fix it.

Their cloaked ship was around the side of the volcano from the rendezvous point. Tabitha, moving quickly, managed to get to a vantage point partway up one of the slopes as soon as she saw the three ships.

The ships had set down on the beach next to the volcano. They were still warmed up, almost as if everyone was ready to escape, and that gave Tabitha an idea.

"Hsst!" The sound carried to her ears, but barely. Tabitha looked around, frowning.

Fuck!

Ryu, Kouki, and Hirotoshi had managed to get out of the conference room somehow. She noticed another figure.

Was that Katsu as well? Dammit.

"Bad Tontos," she muttered to herself as she started back down the slope. "Bad, bad Tontos. Very bad. A thousand push-ups for everyone," she whispered.

She didn't intend to let them do this the "reasonable" way or the "smart" way, either. She wanted to punch a lot of Skaines in the face very hard until their heads exploded.

She wanted the Skaines to be very sorry for what they had done...and then she was going to kill them.

But first, she was going to have a little fun. After all,

three ships full of Skaines was a bit beyond even *her* abilities.

A soft *"Tabitha!"* came from behind her somewhere.

Ignoring the call, she strode onto the beach with her coat pushed back and her Jean Dukes clearly visible, and the Skaines looked around, hands going instantly to their weapons, eyes darting to one another suspiciously.

Good. This was going to be easier than she'd thought.

"'Sup, Blinky?" Tabitha asked the first captain, who kept blinking nervously. His eyes were even more bulbous than the usual specimen's. She looked at the other two, one with *very* blue skin. "Blue. Beans."

"'Beans?'" the third one asked.

"I needed something with a B." She pulled out one of her Jean Dukes and smiled. "Doesn't matter much. You see, Blinky here turned you two in."

"*What?*" The one she called Beans whipped around to glare at Blinky. "You turned us *in*, you snake?"

"I didn't!" Blinky pointed at Tabitha, his fingers shaking. "I swear I didn't! She's lying."

"Snitches get stitches," Tabitha offered with a shrug before Beans and Blue could begin to believe him. "I told you I was going to interrupt the trade. Didn't you think you were going to have to deal with some of the mess?"

Beans and Blue looked at Tabitha, trying to figure out if she was telling the truth. Meanwhile, there was a rustle in the greenery, and Hirotoshi and the others joined her.

"Good, you're here." Tabitha smiled at Hirotoshi, ignoring his stony expression. "Start rounding these bastards up." She pitched her voice a little higher, gesturing vaguely toward the ships with her head.

Dammit, I'm going to have to admit to Achronyx that his help would have been appreciated right now.

She called, "You can let Blinky's crew off the hook, given that he's the one who snitched."

"Hey!" One of the Skaine crew members looked furious. "We get rounded up and *they* get to go free, just because Vel'un snitched?"

Vel'un. Tabitha filed the name away and shrugged, her face the very picture of innocence. "That's how snitching works, kids. If they survive this mess, they get all the rewards."

Vel'un's crew were looking at one another furtively. They weren't sure who Tabitha was, but given the fact that they'd all been nervous about this deal, they were beginning to think maybe she *should* kill everyone else and spare them—and they weren't about to mess with that by saying they didn't deserve it.

"Oh, hell no!" One of the Skaines on another crew rushed at them before they could get their weapons up, and after a few shocked moments the rest of the crews piled on.

"See?" Tabitha called to Hirotoshi.

He glared at her.

Then something like a rocket-propelled grenade soared out of the middle of the fight and headed right toward Tabitha.

"Fucksticks!" Tabitha's eyes got large before she dove sideways.

"Get the captains!" Ryu yelled, and the Tontos charged.

Tabitha laughed hysterically as she launched herself into action.

Near the three ships that were arranged in a semicircle on the beach, there were crates of what she could only assume were drugs and various weapons. Some of the Skaines were running for the crates, either to protect the contents or to use them against their enemies—she wasn't sure which.

But there was also a pen of slaves all chained together, and some of the crew were running for *them.*

There was no good reason for that. Tabitha circled around the main brawl at a sprint and plunged headlong into the back of the group going for the slaves.

She grabbed one particularly ugly Skaine by the arm and swung him around. "Lights out, motherfucker. Don't. Trade. Slaves." She punched him twice in the face so hard his nose shattered under her hand.

Two more had noticed her and they swung around, rocks shooting from under their boots as they slid, grabbing for their weapons.

"Too slow!" Tabitha whipped her Jean Dukes up and shot the first, his chest exploding in gore, but the second was directly between her and the slaves. She charged him, dodging one hasty snap-shot before she got close enough and kneed him between the legs. Then she lashed out and heel-struck him in the temple. He went down and didn't get up again, and she wrenched the gun out of his hands.

She used the gun's stock to bludgeon a few more. After using Jean Dukes' creations, there was no way she was going to shoot a subpar gun unless there was really no other option.

Besides, it was always funny to see their faces when she *hit* them with a gun.

"Don't! Trade! Slaves!" Tabitha yelled as she whipped the gun around and hit one of the Skaines so hard the whole thing bent. He shrieked in pain, and she hauled him up by the neck. "I will find all of you," she promised, her eyes now glowing red, "and I will kill every single one of you slave-trading bastards!"

"I thought you were going to let us live?" one of them blubbered.

So Vel'un was the one trading slaves, then. Tabitha shrugged and pulled out her Jean Dukes again. "Shouldn't listen to Ranger Two unless I promise," she admitted simply and shot him in the face. To the slaves, she added, "Sit tight. I'll have you out of there in just a moment."

"You're not taking our merchandise!" one of the Skaines behind her yelled.

Tabitha turned to him, her teeth lengthening and her eyes flashing red. "That was a mistake, cupcake. People aren't *merchandise*."

Looking around, he seemed to recognize his mistake, and backed away, gulping.

His friends had his back, though. They all stuck close to him, and a few had the sense to raise their weapons. Tabitha threw back her head and laughed and charged into their midst with a battle cry, grabbing a rifle from one and swinging it at anyone and everyone she could reach. Pulling up, she realized she had bent it on someone's head.

"Piece of *crap*," she spat.

"Someone should go check on her!" Katsu yelled from the other side of the battlefield. His sword was coated in blood, and he was grinning savagely as he cut up under an opponent's ribs. The Skaine's scream quickly turned into a gurgle.

"Yes," Ryu agreed. "Someone!" He slid into a deep crouch, using his forward foot to trip an enemy who was making for Katsu. A knife made short work of the fallen alien and he stood up, pivoting on his left foot to slam into an opponent with his right.

The Skaine went over with a wheeze. "But I'm a little busy," Ryu finished. "Hirotoshi?"

"You're not the only one who's busy." Hirotoshi's voice was clipped. His sword flashed in three fast downward strokes, and three Skaines fell. Two screams sounded, and a third's head bounced gently across the sand.

"Anyone want to play volleyball after this?" Ryu asked, watching the head bounce away before splattering against a large rock.

Hirotoshi was trying not to smile. "Perhaps we should deal with the fifty or so angry Skaines we still have left."

"Indeed." Ryu matched his tone mockingly. He pulled his sword and turned to face one of the Skaines who had been trying to sneak up on him. "Hello. You're about to die."

In the midst of the Skaine brawl, Vel'un was repeatedly screaming that he had *not* turned the other two captains in.

Dammit, who *was* this strange alien who had just shown up out of nowhere? She had come to the worst meeting, as far as he was concerned. He had just gotten Klik'ad and Droze to accept that he was worth trading with, and the *first* deal went wrong?

It was some weird twist of fate, and he hated it. He was a good, honest trader. He never shorted his buyers, and his slaves were good quality, all taken from reasonable colonies with good nutrition. He *never* passed off weak, near-dead inventory like *some* of his people did.

What had he ever done to deserve this? *Nothing.*

When he came face to face with one of the humans, he shrieked in fury.

"Whoever you are, leave me *alone!*" He stomped his foot.

"*No,*" the human replied instantly. It didn't seem at all inclined to bargain with him. "You are a slave trader, and you will be judged as one."

"Judged?" *What the hell did that mean?* Vel'un wondered. "I haven't cheated anyone! They can tell you my prices are fair."

"You are being judged," Hirotoshi told him, "for trading slaves at all. It is an abhorrent practice that our Empress forbids."

"Your Empress…" Vel'un could barely speak, he was so shocked and angry. They were beyond the borders of the Etheric Empire! How could that bitch hope to enforce laws out here?

Then he looked at the humans and realized that *they* were the way she was hoping to enforce laws.

"Skaines!" He raised his voice. "Skaines, stop fighting each other! Fight the humans!"

"Stop yelling," Hirotoshi told him. He reached out and dragged the Skaine close, putting handcuffs on him and throwing him away from the battle. "When this is over, if you have survived, you will be judged."

"This isn't legal!" Vel'un yelled.

"In many cases, there is a difference between what is

legal and what is right." Hirotoshi looked at him gravely. "We do not accept your laws."

He slid into action once more, dragging individuals away from the brawl between the ships' crews and cutting their throats with his knives or breaking their necks. He did not use his sword for this. He would use that only in combat, where his opponent could attack, facing him. Something in him still did not like picking opponents off one by one.

It felt dishonest.

With the odds so stacked against them, however, and their opponents holding the slaves hostage, he would not let minor points of etiquette hold him back from doing what was right.

Vel'un was still yelling for the Skaines to stop fighting one another and start fighting the humans, however, and some of them were taking notice. Fistfights between the crews began to clear up, however grudgingly, and the Skaines turned to face the Tontos and Tabitha.

A ship screamed overhead, and everyone looked up to see the QBS *Augustus* hovering just behind the three Skaine ships.

"Just making sure none of them decide to run," Jun said in their implants.

The humans below nodded.

Katsu was looking around. "We're missing one of the captains. I don't know where he hid, but he managed to."

"We'll find him," Hirotoshi told him.

"Was it Beans or Blue?" Ryu asked.

"Beans," Katsu told them.

"Not important right now," Hirotoshi reported. "They are all facing us now."

"Surround and conquer." Ryu drew his sword and settled into a fighting stance.

"Surround and conquer?" the other four echoed.

"Kill the motherfuckers," Tabitha added succinctly. "Chaaaaaarge!"

"Anyone who stands down—" Hirotoshi began, but Tabitha cut him off.

"Hell, no! I do NOT agree to that!"

"*Kemosabe*," Hirotoshi shot back. He could see Ryu, Kouki, and Katsu staring at him with shocked looks on their faces. They had never seen him countermand one of Tabitha's orders in this way, or try to take control of a situation.

However, in this case, he worried that Tabitha's grief might drive her to do things that she would later regret.

He figured she could always kill the Skaines after the fight if it turned out they needed killing. She couldn't un-kill them if the reverse turned out to be true.

The Skaines decided to force his hand, however. Of the fifty or so left, ten decided to rush Tabitha at once, and Hirotoshi slid into action immediately.

"Hai!" He sliced up, to take the attacker closest to him, and then down, pulling up quickly to avoid lodging his sword in the Skaine's collarbone.

Katsu and Ryu circled around to the back of the group. The other Skaines were still hanging back, having apparently decided to take Hirotoshi at his word. A few of them had put guns on the ground.

Tabitha had dispatched the first and second attackers

and was currently sidestepping a third, who had run at her with a knife. She lashed out at him with her elbow as he stumbled past her and grabbed his arm, breaking the joint with her other hand and catching the knife when it fell from his nerveless fingers.

"I don't know why you bothered," she called to Hirotoshi. "None of them will do anything other than try to kill us."

Hirotoshi and Katsu spun in unison, cutting down the last two attackers, and Hirotoshi nodded deeply to Tabitha.

"I apologize for speaking out of turn, Kemosabe."

Tabitha opened her mouth and closed it. Adrenaline was still pumping through her blood from the fight, and she realized she wasn't done fighting yet. She wanted to feel the impact of her fist against a few more faces.

She was almost angry enough at everything to want one of those faces to be Hirotoshi's. These Skaines were hardly a challenge, after all. She wanted a *real* sparring session.

And she wanted to take one of those swords and lay into the rest of the group.

They had known.

They had been well aware of the kind of trade they were getting into, and she wasn't just going to stand by and watch them get away with it while Shin—

She looked around, struggling for calm.

Hirotoshi, wisely, did not approach her. It was Ryu, still cleaning his blade, who came to stand next to her to survey the group.

"There is one captain to judge at the moment," he told her. "Over there." He nodded to the left. "Hirotoshi tied him up and left him for you. The other...we don't know.

They set up the deals, though. Every captain here was complicit in that trade." His voice went to a murmur and he nodded toward the slaves, adding, "We need to figure out how to get them somewhere safe, too."

Tabitha managed to nod. The mention of the slaves steadied her. What they needed was to get the chains off and get somewhere that they could rebuild their lives or get safe passage home—and hopefully keep themselves safe until she'd managed to wipe out every Skaine bastard in the universe.

What they *didn't* need was to witness a bloodbath.

She went over to Vel'un first and pushed him onto his back with her boot. "You. Start talking."

He glared up at her. "What I did was perfectly legal. You have no right to—"

"Wrong answer." Tabitha's eyes went red, and she hauled him up by his neck. He choked and spluttered as she pulled him close to her face. "Where did you find these slaves? And remember, they're right there and I can ask *them*."

"On some mining colonies," Vel'un spat. "I can't breathe."

"Maybe I should put one of those collars on *you*." But Tabitha dropped him to the sand with a sound of disgust. "So you went in, captured them, and were going to sell them, and you want me to believe that's just totally legal, and *furthermore*, that you see no problem with it at all?"

"It…" Well, it was a gray area, taking people from sovereign colonies. "I don't see anything wrong with it!"

"That's disgusting," Tabitha held back the kick she so desperately wanted to give him. "You're slime. Skaines like you are the reason I'm here, ridding the galaxy of *every single one of you fuckers* I find. You aren't the first, and you won't be the last." She pulled out her Jean Dukes and fired. "You have been judged as guilty. No one will remember you," she told his body. "And that was for Shin."

"Kemosabe," Ryu called. "We found the last captain."

He and Hirotoshi dragged forward two Skaines who had evidently been hiding amongst the slaves, holding them hostage with sidearms and telling them not to make a sound and betray that they were there.

They were thrown onto the ground in front of Tabitha, and she stared down at them with distaste.

"*Well?*"

"I'm innocent!" the Skaine protested. "I didn't know what Vel'un was up to! I'd told him I wanted to call off the trade because it was slaves, and then you showed up."

"I think that's a big fat lie," Tabitha said sweetly. "A *really* big fat lie. Just as big a lie as Vel'un saying he didn't see anything wrong with trading slaves."

"He was the one who called you on us, though!"

Ah, yes. *That* lie. Tabitha didn't want to expose Guildert, either. They might need him again. "Well, that was an error in judgment on Vel'un's part, wasn't it? He thought you were going to cheat him."

"Cheat him? For *that* lousy stock?" The captain looked at the slaves contemptuously. "They're all skinny and weak, and…" His voice trailed off in horror as he realized what he had admitted.

"Uh-huh." Tabitha shot him and turned to the other Skaine. "Who's this?"

"The first mate, I'm guessing." Ryu rolled his eyes. "He's blubbering too much for us to tell, though."

The first mate was, indeed, crying big crocodile tears as he wailed something only half-intelligible about how he hadn't known, or maybe he had known, but what could you do? Times were so hard these days.

Tabitha shot him and sighed as the body hit the ground.

"What do we do with this lot?" she asked no one in particular.

"The QBS *Nor'easter* is close enough," Hirotoshi suggested. "They should have both the space and the time to get these people back to their homes, or bring them somewhere else safe."

"Oh, right." Tabitha looked at the slaves. "No, I meant *them.*" She nodded to the rest of the Skaines. "I say we take them with the slaves and us, but in a different ship...that maybe 'accidentally' gets vented into space."

"Kemosabe." Hirotoshi's face was grave. "It was one thing to fight the crew before they surrendered. Now they have, however, and unlike the others, they are not attacking you. To commit wholesale murder..."

Tabitha sank her face into her hands and rubbed at it for a while, working on herself before looking up with a different light in her eyes. "Right. I won't stain Shin's memory with unethical actions as a Ranger."

Tabitha stalked over to the group of Skaines and her lip curled as they flinched away from her. She put up two fingers, just an inch apart. "But *please, please* try me just a little, and I will *accidentally* backhand your head off your shoulders so fast you will blink your eyes as you watch your body collapse. *Capisce?*"

They might not know Italian, but they all knew when to nod.

Tabitha made a disgusted noise and nodded to the Tontos. "Let's get the slaves onto the *Augustus*. I'd give them a Skaine ship, but I'm not sure they'd know how to fly it. And if they were held captive on one…"

"It might be the last place they want to be now," Katsu finished, understanding. "I will begin loading them onto the ship." He waved at Jun to land as Hirotoshi began giving orders to the Skaines.

Those orders were sprinkled liberally with reminders not to attempt to evade the Empress' orders against slavery "on pain of death."

"On pain of *pain*," Tabitha muttered to herself as she strode up the gangway into the *Augustus*. "I'm not just going to kill them if they throw away this chance. I'm going to make it *hurt*."

She expected a snarky response from Achronyx, but of course, Achronyx wasn't here. She sighed and crossed her arms, and looked at Jun as he made his way down the hall toward her.

"What is it, Kemosabe?"

"We're going to get the *Achronyx* back," Tabitha told him. "It's our ship. I don't like working with this loaner. It's a fine ship," she added hastily, for some reason worried that she would hurt its feelings, "but the *Achronyx* is home."

CHAPTER 10 NICKIE

Rebus Quadrant, Aboard the *Penitent Granddaughter*, Main Galley

Carefully, Grim topped off the last bowl from one of the several pots he had been cooking in. It had all gone considerably smoother once he was aware that some Skaine spices spontaneously combusted. Plus, he had someone who actually spoke Skaine with him helping out now.

He and Durq were loading the food onto a few carts when Nickie poked her head in from the corridor. Durq scuttled away and hid in the closet when Nickie stepped the rest of the way into the room.

Grim kept loading the carts. "Perfect timing. You can help me deliver these."

"Uh, no?" Nickie corrected immediately, shaking her head. "I don't do manual labor. That's not on my résumé."

Grim eyed her for a moment, frowning.

"We were just at a space station," he pointed out.

"Weren't you specifically supposed to be finding people to do some of the heavy lifting while we were there?"

Nickie cleared her throat. "I did," she replied primly. She clapped her hands and, beeping and buzzing, the four new house bots bumbled into the kitchen behind her. "Meet Meredith's new minions!" She threw her hands out to her sides with all the flair of a stage magician. "Pretty fucking great, aren't they?"

Grim didn't answer, and it became apparent that he wasn't paying an ounce of attention to her. He stared at the bots, mandibles flaring slightly as he tried to figure out something to say. Finally, he simply plopped on the floor and started cooing over the nearest one.

"I'll call you Brandy," he informed the copper-colored one and laughed in delight when it continued loading the carts for him. The silver one, the gold one, and the red one (summarily dubbed Lefty, Lucky, and Bradley respectively) trundled in its wake to help.

Nickie watched for a few moments in disbelief before ducking out of the kitchen again. She had only made it a few steps down the corridor when Grim called after her. "You know we're still going to need your help, right?"

Nickie kicked the wall with one foot, mumbling, "Sonofabitch," under her breath.

"My mother was a lovely woman," Grim replied, poking his head out of the kitchen. "And someone needs to make sure none of the Skaines get out while the food's being delivered. That, I'm sure, *is* on your résumé."

Nickie wasted a few more seconds muttering under her breath before she reluctantly agreed, still grumbling, "I *told* you I don't fucking do manual labor," as she trudged after Grim and the bots.

"And now you do," he returned pleasantly, sparing her not a single ounce of sympathy.

Rebus Quadrant, Aboard the *Penitent Granddaughter*

Nickie shoved the empty cart back into the galley with a bit more force than was strictly necessary. She didn't feel a bit of remorse when she heard Durq yelp in surprise. She wasn't sure where Grim had wandered off to in the two minutes since she had last seen him, but she was pretty sure she was going to kill him when she got her hands on him. She was exhausted.

You did at least get to know your new ship to some extent.

Meredith didn't seem to have any sympathy for Nickie's plight either.

I could have just looked at the maps, Nickie grumbled in return. *I didn't need to walk the whole fucking rig, and it's not like I need the cardio.*

Meredith didn't reply immediately, but Nickie got the impression that the EI wished she had eyes to roll.

We have roughly two hours until we can drop off the Skaines.

Nickie waved a hand in vague acknowledgment and turned toward the bridge. When she got there, she found Grim setting up dinner on what looked to be a folding card table and a pair of stools. Simple food, but considerably better than what Nickie might find in a can in the back of a cupboard. And more importantly, there were two glasses and a bottle of Yollin whiskey.

Silently, Nickie reconsidered her determination to kill

him. Instead, she dropped onto one of the stools. There was no fanfare as they started eating.

"So, what next?" Grim wondered after a minute.

"We drop off our cargo," Nickie told him. Her gaze focused on the distance as she brought up the Skaine job database on her HUD. It was bustling with activity still. "And…we deal with some of the shadier goings-on, I think."

Grim sulked at her as he groused, "Do we need to talk about that while we're eating?"

"Slave-trading, weapons-trading, mercenary operations…" Nickie mused as she scrolled through the listings, ignoring Grim's protests. "It's all pretty fucking gross, yeah?" She didn't wait for a reply. "So, we should do something about it. Just…you know, productively."

"Productively?" Grim paused with a fork raised halfway to his mouth for a second before he carried on eating.

Nickie heaved a sigh. "Look, if I'm going to be doing vigilante work, I would at least like to turn some sort of a profit from it. It's not like anyone's going to pay me a goddamn thing if I just blow whoever picks up a job to pieces and then whoosh on my way."

Grim held up his free hand in a placating gesture. "Far be it from me to tell you how to be a vigilante, but what do you have in mind?"

"I mean, we're *on* a Skaine ship," Nickie replied, gesturing around with one hand. "The system has all the relevant flags and markers. Meredith is just masking them. We could totally accept jobs, demand part of the payment upfront, and then fuck everything to high hell once we're on site."

Grim hummed a contemplative note. "Wouldn't the ship get blacklisted fairly quickly?"

Nickie opened her mouth to reply, but Meredith cut her off.

"I can scramble the ship's identification beacon between jobs," she supplied. "As far as the system is concerned, a different ship would be applying each time."

"So then we get paid to ship a bunch of slaves or whatever it might be at the time, show up, free the slaves and start a revolution, and then we fly off into the night," Nickie concluded. "And no one will ever be the wiser about who we actually are."

"Unless you decide to dramatically announce yourself again," Grim remarked dryly.

"Look," Nickie pointed her fork at his face, right between his mandibles, "I needed a dramatic moment, and the stationmaster had it coming."

"If you say so." He returned his attention to his meal. "I can't argue with freeing slaves anyway, even if we probably won't actually start any revolutions."

"The plan is foolproof," Nickie assured him, picking up the bottle and pouring herself a healthy amount of whiskey. "Or at least fairly workable, and that's good enough for me."

That determination made, she picked up her glass, threw her head back, and drained it in one long swig.

Rebus Quadrant, Aboard the *Penitent Granddaughter*

The ship slowed as it approached the docks of Memento Luna.

Approaching with caution was probably unwarranted.

The planet wasn't exactly well-armed, and it wasn't prone to violence. By the time the *Granddaughter* had docked, the worst that had happened was that Meredith had had to fudge a few reports to satisfy the docking master

She noted dryly to Nickie that his title seemed a little grand, given the circumstances.

As Grim cleaned up from dinner, Nickie mused, "It's a pretty low-tech colony. Pretty unlikely any of them will be able to radio off the planet unless a ship is basically on top of them, and no one ever comes here. There's nothing to really hurt them unless they turn on each other, so they'll all be as snug as bugs in a lot of really ugly rugs on the planet with no way to come after us."

"Are you done assuring yourself you're not murdering them all through neglect?" Grim wondered. "Because if we don't get finished quickly, the docking master is probably going to come see what we're here for even with Meredith running interference. Small colonies are nosy."

Nickie rolled her eyes. "Yeah, yeah. Meredith, patch me through to the ship-wide intercom," she instructed, pulling her communicator out. She waited until she could see the patch-in process complete in the corner of her vision before she began to speak.

"To the several dozen Skaines still in residence on *my ship*," she began, emphasizing her ownership as emphatically as she could without holding up a neon sign. "We're now docked on Memento Luna. To anyone who doesn't know, it's a tiny little spit of a colony at the ass-end of nowhere. Communication is limited, and it gets a single commercial trading vessel each solar year."

She started pacing across the bridge as she spoke. "My

research tells me there are only three months to go until this year's vessel shows up. So just hold out 'til then, avoid getting eaten by a feral Tamagotchi or whatever, get picked up, and you should all be happily home in…eh, about five months, give or take. So get ready to disembark, and remember that if you try to break my ship, I will step on you."

Satisfied, Nickie turned off her communicator and shoved it back into her jacket. Almost immediately, Grim's communicator went off instead. Nickie stared at him for the entire duration of the brief conversation, if it could even be called a conversation. Grim hardly said anything until the end, and then his only contribution was a bland, "Yeah, all right," before he hung up.

"Durq would rather stay on the ship," he informed Nickie as he tucked his communicator away again. "He would rather take his chances here with us than on the colony with everyone else."

"Durq?"

Grim sighed. "Skaine. Small. Probably still hiding in the closet in the galley. You pulled him out of the room beside the galley earlier today."

Come with me if you want to live, Meredith repeated crossly. *Really?*

"Oh, right." The name sort of rang a bell. "And…why do I care what he'd prefer?" she asked flatly, her eyebrows rising.

"Because letting him get eaten is cruel and would shunt you from 'vigilante' to 'psychopath,'" Grim reasoned like a teacher explaining where a math equation went wrong. "Besides, if we're going to pretend to be a Skaine ship, we should probably have a Skaine on board that we can show people if they get suspicious."

"But he's a *Skaine*," Nickie protested. Her tone only avoided whining by a very slim margin. "Having one around is just asking for trouble."

"You'll probably barely see him," Grim replied as he leaned down to hand the dishes from dinner to Brandy and Lefty. "I figure he'll just stay in the galley or his own room most of the time."

"And it would be useful to actually have a Skaine aboard a Skaine ship," Meredith agreed. "He's not wrong in that regard."

Nickie groaned when the pair of them ganged up on her, and she slumped into the command chair. "Fiiiiine." She huffed, folding her arms over her chest. "He can stay. But I don't have to like it. And it's not for him. It's just so we can use him as a front man," she insisted sharply.

"Your generous sacrifice will be remembered," Grim assured her, feigning as much earnestness as he could manage while still keeping a straight face. "Anything you need me to do before we drop off all the other Skaines?"

Heaving a sigh, Nickie shook her head. "No, not really," she replied glumly, sliding lower in her seat. "Meredith and I can handle it."

"Mostly me," Meredith chimed in through the speakers. As Grim tried and failed to muffle a snort of laughter behind his hands, Nickie waved both middle fingers at the ceiling.

The dock at Memento Luna could scarcely be dignified with the term, really. It was open-air and tiny, with only enough space for four ships considerably smaller than the *Penitent Granddaughter* to dock at once, so the *Granddaughter* wound up occupying two spaces.

Nickie felt a bit like they were double-parked, regardless of the necessity.

There were docking workers, of course. The colony was too low-tech for the entire matter to be automated. But there were only a handful of them, and when Nickie tuned into their radio chatter, they all sounded like they were minimum-wage students working through a school break. It seemed that an unscheduled battleship dropping into orbit was the most exciting thing that had happened in months, and Nickie wasn't even surprised. The workers nearly went bonkers when a hoard of surly Skaines started filing out of the ship like the galaxy's angriest colony of ants.

The Skaines being unloaded weren't pleased about the conditions of the colony, and they made their thoughts known as they shouted and raged and picked senseless fights with each other as if Nickie would change her mind if they just kicked up enough of a fuss.

As if.

Truth be told, she was hardly paying them any attention, other than the bare minimum awareness to make sure they weren't trying to break part of the ship as a last act of rebellion. Instead, she was comfortably squirreled away on the bridge.

The doors to the bridge were locked, so none of the Skaines could get in. Even if they could, Meredith was only letting them off one room at a time. Nickie wasn't particularly concerned about a room's worth of Skaines coming after her, and all of them so far had made the wise choice to simply leave without making a fuss.

It helped that Lucky and Bradley were patrolling the corridors. They had both acquired their own tasers. Nickie wasn't sure where the tasers had come from, but she decided it was probably good they were armed. Saved her the hassle of stepping in.

So far, only two of the Skaines had been shocked and left drooling on the floor for a few minutes, and that seemed to have been enough of a warning to the others not to try any sort of funny business.

Meredith and the bots were handling the unloading of the Skaines without her.

And since her help didn't seem to be needed, she instead sat around on the bridge of the ship scrolling idly through the job database.

Besides, she was refusing to actually look up for the time being. Despite Grim's assurance that Durq would probably stay in the galley most of the time, he was *right there* on the other side of the bridge, partially hidden under a terminal and watching the unloading proceedings on the main viewing screen.

"There's a slave shipment that's supposed to be picked up not far from here," she observed eventually, glancing in Grim's direction. "Headcount of at least a few hundred, and a pretty hefty payout for transport." She paused for a split second to see if he had any sort of reaction to the news. "We've got plenty of time to interrupt them. The planet is in this quadrant."

Grim's eyes narrowed in thought, and his mandibles pulled close to his mouth. "Are you sure that's the best idea when there are only three of us?" he asked after a few seconds of thought. "It's not like we're armed to the teeth or anything." His mandibles twitched as he cautioned her, "Maybe we should wait to be vigilantes until after we have a crew?"

Nickie scoffed. "Please, I count for at *least* fifty people on my own, so there are fifty-two of us."

There was a beat as her gaze fell on Durq. He blinked at her before withdrawing farther back into his hiding spot under the terminal. She was pretty sure he squeaked in alarm, like a chew toy one gave to pets.

"Fifty-one and a half," she amended, turning her attention back to the database. "That's a perfectly respectable crew, and anyway, this is a *battleship*. I'm pretty sure I can find some goddamned weapons on board. Plus, I could get creative."

Grim shrugged, conceding the point without an argument. He wasn't the sort to bash his head against a brick wall recreationally.

Nickie grinned triumphantly and bookmarked the information on the trade. Her eyes slid to the side as Meredith chimed in.

The last of the Skaines are off of the ship. I've run a scan to make sure we don't have any stowaways other than Durq, and there were no notable incidents to report. Shall I pull the ship out of the dock?

The results of the scan appeared in the corner of Nickie's vision.

Make it so! Nickie confirmed. She tapped her finger

against the offer in the database. *And here are our next coordinates.*

I'll do my best to make the approach subtle.

Nickie almost wanted to caution her to make sure the *exit* was subtle, considering how tightly the ship was cramped into the dock and how likely it seemed that they could take out half the dock with one wrong move. She kept the thought to herself, though, less because she knew Meredith could handle any sort of maneuver than because she figured it would be funny as hell if something *did* happen.

As the ship began to pull out of the dock Nickie looked at the primary viewing screen, where the gaggle of Skaines was milling about in irritated bemusement. The continued chatter of the dock workers made it seem like a scene straight out of a really bad comedy.

Nickie bowed with a flourish and waved at the screen. "So long, farewell, goodbye, and all that other bullshit. I'd say I'll never forget our time together, but the details are already getting fuzzy. Glad to have you out of my hair, scumbags!"

She waved one middle finger at the screen.

Grim watched her like he wasn't quite sure whether he thought she was funny or just exasperating. She grinned at him over her shoulder.

"You ready to blow this pop stand?" she asked brightly, settling back in her seat.

He shook his head. "As ready as I'll ever be, as long as you're finished with your dramatics."

Nickie scoffed and flapped a hand at him. "Yeah, right. Not fucking likely."

CHAPTER 11 TABITHA

They rendezvoused with the QBS *Nor'easter* a few hours later. The captain, a woman named Jane Kelly, was surprisingly open to a detour that would bring them into the system.

The reason for the detour was made clear not long after Tabitha came on board. Kelly's crew was moving the slaves to the spare living quarters, and Kelly herself came to take Tabitha and the Tontos to the viewing deck.

A ship floated outside, looking fresh from production. Its paint was shiny and it had a red stripe across the bow, and Tabitha looked at it curiously. It looked familiar, but—

She did a double-take.

ACHRONYX?

Hello, Ranger Two, Achronyx replied smugly.

The Tontos had also identified the ship and were laughing and nodding their approval.

As you can see, Achronyx told them all, *the repairs went very well.*

Yeah, I'm glad you took this chance to get your face fixed, Tabitha joked. *You weren't looking so good.*

Ryu smirked, and Achronyx sat in stony silence.

"It was explained to us," Captain Kelly said, "that we could tow or crew the *Augustus*, and you could continue on your travels on the *Achronyx*."

"Sounds great!" Tabitha agreed. She shook Kelly's hand. "Nice to meet you. We'll go transfer over our stuff."

I don't know, Achronyx interjected stiffly. *Perhaps Ranger Two does not want an old broken-down ship like me around.*

Oh, come on, Achronyx. Tabitha chuckled as she made her way down the corridor. *I have nothing but respect for your abilities as an EI and a ship.*

Achronyx waited, ready to be mollified.

You're just as ugly as sin, Tabitha told him cheerfully. *That red stripe really distracts the eye, though, so that's good.*

Kemosabe, Hirotoshi interjected, *please do not provoke Achronyx. I do not want to be flown into the side of a planet.*

You're worse than she is! Achronyx accused. *She insults my looks. You insult my calling as an EI. I would never dishonor myself by killing my crew.*

Everyone settle down, Tabitha ordered. *We're just kidding with you, Achronyx.*

Achronyx grumbled, but docked and allowed them all to come aboard with their things.

Knowing that Achronyx was grumpy, Tabitha and the Tontos made a big deal of all the new upgrades. The ship had been cleaned inside and out, and many improvements had been made beyond new paint and giving the ship a new hull.

It was good to be home.

As they worked with some of the crew, one of the previous slaves came up to her.

"I wanted to thank you." Uleg was moving his weight from one leg to another. "To have someone come and stand up for us...it means a lot. When we were captured, we were taken from a poor colony. They had no resources to come find us and fight for us, or even buy us back. We thought we would never see our homes again." He clasped Tabitha's hand in both of his. "Thank you. *Thank you.*"

Tabitha nodded awkwardly, then, surprised, allowed herself to be hugged. After he left, she walked back to the ship in silence with Hirotoshi beside her.

"Is something wrong?" he asked her.

She frowned at the question. "I don't know." She glanced over her shoulder briefly. "Well, yes I do. I didn't do what I did for *them*. I did it for Shin."

Hirotoshi said nothing. He waited, his face passive, as the blast doors closed and the ships began to undock from one another.

She continued talking. "I wanted to kill *all* of the Skaines for what they did to him. I guess I still do. I just feel like I should be doing it for the slaves, too." Tabitha lifted one shoulder and looked at him. "But I'm not. I just don't... It's not that I don't care at all. I just don't care as much as I think I should."

Hirotoshi considered this as they began to walk back to the bridge. "Perhaps it is part of the same thing," he suggested finally. "Kemosabe, you are angry at the Skaines—"

"That's enough of an understatement to be inaccurate," Tabitha quipped.

Hirotoshi smiled. "You want to root them out because they hurt people. Because they hurt *you*. You don't have to care about Shin *or* the slaves. You can care for both. So many of these people have also lost loved ones to the Skaines."

Tabitha stopped at the door of her rooms, thinking about this piece of advice. Hirotoshi gave a little bow and walked away, leaving her to her thoughts. He had seen enough death in his years not to fall prey to the feeling Tabitha had now: the desire for blind vengeance.

He would step in, as he had on the planet, to gently guide her away from actions he thought she would regret.

But he knew the only way forward for her was to grieve for Shin in her own way.

In her rooms, Tabitha settled into a deep chair and considered Hirotoshi's words.

I'm glad to be back, Achronyx, she said finally. *I was just telling Kouki before we took off from the planet that I wanted to go back and get you.*

Is that so, Ranger Two? Achronyx sounded wary, as if he suspected her of making a joke at his expense.

Yes, Achronyx, it is. Tabitha stood up and went to the side of the bed, where there was a picture of her with the Tontos. She had taken to looking away from it when she got up each day, and whoever had cleaned the ship had polished the glass.

She stared at the picture for a long time.

"I miss him," she finally admitted aloud. "You get used

to war, Achronyx. You think because you've pulled things off before..." She bit her lip. "I left the Tontos on the ship on the last mission. I thought my plans had gotten someone killed. I didn't want them to get hurt following me."

Achronyx said nothing, waiting in silence. It was, oddly, the perfect way to comfort her.

"I miss him," Tabitha repeated. She put the picture frame face-down on the bedside table and went to change. "Head back to Farha Station, Achronyx. We're still hunting Skaines."

Farha Station

Tabitha, Katsu, and Hirotoshi swept into Guildert's offices on Farha Station a day later. They had taken their time with the journey since Hirotoshi pointed out that they still had plenty of time before the "smart virus" was supposed to activate.

"Don't you think we should just let him figure it out on his own?" Tabitha asked.

"No. Remember, you wanted to keep him as an informant," Hirotoshi pointed out.

"Oh. Right. Why is the fun thing never the *smart* thing to do?"

"Surely a question for the ages." Hirotoshi looked like he was close to rolling his eyes.

"Keep being snarky, Number One, and see where it gets you in sparring."

Hirotoshi did grin at that, and they had gotten to work on planning their next steps.

However, when they got to Guildert's offices, they

found that the Torcellan had already determined what the "smart virus" really was, and he was *not* pleased about the whole affair.

"I spent considerable time and effort," he ground out, tight-lipped, "on determining what, exactly, had been put into my blood, only to find out that my information was given under false pretenses. It was an inert compound!"

"Are you sure about that?" Hirotoshi held up another syringe, his face bland. "Because that's quite a gamble."

"Not a gamble at all," Guildert told him angrily. "I have access to the best scientists in the sector, thank you very much. And do you know why I needed to do that? Because accidents happen, and if you had died, I would have died with you for no good reason! Or so I thought." He sniffed and settled back in his chair. The lights woven into his silvery hair cast tiny shadows on his face.

"Yeah, *Hirotoshi.*" Tabitha elbowed him. "That was really rude. You should apologize."

"*You* threatened my life," Guildert told her, sounding outraged that she had not already offered an apology.

"That is *also* considered rude," Hirotoshi told Tabitha gravely.

"Oh. Right. Well, in my defense, I still haven't ever met an honest information broker. You gave us *way* more than we asked for, dude. Was the sex tape really necessary?"

Katsu closed his eyes in pain at the memory of seeing the video.

"I believed I was bargaining for my life!" Guildert slammed his hand down on the table. "No. This is too much. You have to go. I will not deal with you any further."

"But we have more Skaines to find," Tabitha explained.

"Then go speak to Don Guido," Guildert snapped. He saw their faces and sighed. "He's at Yeven's Bar on Level Fifteen, and yes, he already knows who you are, and no, I don't suggest you cheat him."

"I would never cheat someone named Guido," Tabitha told him after a moment. "That's just a *really* bad idea."

The Tontos nodded seriously. Some things were apparently universal amongst humans, even vampires who had spent most of their lives in Japan and Australia.

Guildert gave them a totally baffled look, but he snapped back into fighting form a moment later. "And now I must ask you to leave." He threw an arm out and pointed at the door. "I will not suffer your presence any longer."

"Yeah, yeah," Tabitha grumbled as they filed out the door. "Now, this Guido guy—"

The door slammed, and they stared at it for a moment.

"It's just hard to take him seriously when he has Christmas lights in his hair," Katsu commented finally, and two others snickered.

They set off toward Level Fifteen.

Achronyx, can you find me information on Yeven's Bar and someone named Don Guido? Theoretically an information broker?

Are you pulling my leg?

No, I swear to God that's his name. Hirotoshi, back me up.

That was *what Guildert said,* Hirotoshi agreed. After a moment, he added, *I was surprised, too.*

I'll do what I can. Achronyx sounded doubtful, and Tabitha could hardly blame him. She was wondering if the whole thing was a joke, but it just didn't seem possible that

Guildert would know enough about humans to make a joke like that.

There were always mysteries, she supposed.

They found the bar named "Yeven" on the far end of the fifteenth level. It was packed, which made it a little less creepy, but it was altogether just as sticky as the last bar, and there was the smell of the liquor they'd first been given on this station.

Tabitha and Hirotoshi wrinkled their noses. Katsu, who had not yet been privileged to drink it, didn't notice. Tabitha, noticing this, leaned over to Hirotoshi.

"You should buy him one of those drinks," she muttered out of the side of her mouth.

"I will not," Hirotoshi replied calmly. "I would not inflict such a thing on an ally."

"You're no fun, you know that?" She leaned back.

They got their drinks and went to a booth in the back. No one seemed to take exception to Hirotoshi's face this time, so they had plenty of time to sip their drinks and observe the other patrons.

Tabitha, once she had discerned that what she had was the *good* liquor, downed hers as fast as she could and lifted her empty glass to get another. She smacked her lips as a Torcellan waitress wove between the tables to set it down and take her money.

"Mmm, mmm. I bet this could get me drunk."

"I'll put a bet against," Katsu offered gravely.

"I'll put a bet for," Hirotoshi replied after a moment. "It is *highly* alcoholic, and her nanites have not encountered many drinks of this type before."

"You two have yourselves a deal." Tabitha drained her

second drink and held the glass up again. "Although... Dammit, I have to pee. Do you think there's a bathroom in this place?" She hiccupped, then her eyes narrowed. "If the seat is sticky, I'm using the owner's tongue to clean it."

Yoll Quadrant, QBSS *Meredith Reynolds*, Never Submit-Never Surrender Bar

"Which is as good a stopping point as any," Tabitha rolled her head around. She looked at her beer and tapped the glass. "That's the problem with being a vampire and trying to drink. You don't get buzzed easily, and by the time you do... Well, it's a matter of volume. I'll be back."

She winked at Angie and left, her hips swaying under the black coat. Even though it covered her figure, it wasn't hard to imagine how everything must look in the tight leather pants underneath.

Angie stared after her, wide-eyed, and Terrence laughed.

"Tabitha's not shy," he told her.

George chimed in, "No, she's not."

Angie smiled and took a sip of her beer. She'd been so caught up in listening to Tabitha's story that she had hardly drunk any of it, and it was getting warm.

"I had no idea about the stories Tabitha must have," she said finally. "This is only one of them. Imagine living your whole life like that, out there sticking up for Justice!"

"Don't you do that?" George asked, eyeing her quizzically.

"Yeah," Lilah chimed in. "Tabitha told us you were a gunnery officer."

Angie laughed until she saw that they were all serious.

"I mean, I am," she explained. "But I don't do *anything* like what Tabitha does. She's off tracking people down and bringing them to Justice. I just, you know, make sure all the ordnance is in the right place, and that people know how to use it, and…all of that."

"So, in other words, you help keep our ships in the air and help our enemies get dead," Lilah summarized succinctly. "I'd say you're out there sticking up for Justice as well."

The regulars chorused their agreement and clinked glasses, and Angie clinked hers with theirs shyly.

"So tell us about you," Terrence suggested. "You must have had some close calls, right?"

"Oh, ummm." Angie's eyes lit up. "There was one engagement where they were just zipping around the ship, and we couldn't tell when to fire which guns. When they'd come in range, even for a moment, we'd be firing so fast that the barrels were jamming. Well, I knew that was going to end poorly, so I had people start firing randomly. We couldn't keep up with the fighters, right? So we just cleared our fighters out of the way and started having a whole set of guns firing, but never the same set twice. *That* scared them right off, I tell you. They'd been thinking they were so special, zipping around, but once they knew they might get in the way of a blast and there was no way to anticipate it? They fucked right off. So we were able to get the supplies to the colony we were going to once we got them out of our way."

"There." Terrence patted the table. "See? You've been doing good stuff."

"I have." Angie was buoyed by their cheer, but a

moment later she remembered why she was here listening to this story and her face fell. "But I lost Manny—my boyfriend—and I just don't know what to do with myself these days. My work doesn't seem important anymore. He made everything come alive, and without him, things are… a bit gray, I'd have to admit."

"Hey, now." Tabitha had come back. She nudged Angie with her elbow. "No calling yourself boring. Manny made the world interesting because that was the world *he* saw. You said he cooked, right? It's like that. You see the ingredients. He saw the dish."

"I like thinking of it that way." Angie nodded. Was it possible that the best way she could remember Manny would be to see the world as happily and as interestedly as he had?

Angie took a moment to think how *she* had been holding herself back from experiences because she knew she would want to tell Manny about them.

When she'd first realized she was going to be talking to Ranger Two, her first thought had been sadness that he wouldn't hear about it. She had wanted to turn around and walk away.

He would have been so sad if she had done that. She blinked away tears.

Tabitha, seeing this, motioned to the others to ignore it, but they were already finding any excuse to look elsewhere. This group looked out for one another. They weren't going to embarrass the new girl by pointing out that she was crying.

"So, where was I?" Tabitha asked vaguely.

"You were in a bar," Angie reminded her, sniffing and wiping her nose on a bar napkin.

"Oh, right. The bar fight."

"No, you already told me the bit about the bar fight."

"Oh, you precious little unicorn." Terrence reached out to put his hand over Angie's. "None of Tabitha's stories have just *one* bar fight."

Angie started laughing, and Tabitha gave Terrence an approving nod. *Good job making her laugh.*

"He's right," she told Angie. "There are more bar fights. For instance, the one with Don Guido."

"I meant to ask about that." Angie hadn't been born on Earth, but some jokes traveled just fine, what with all the movies people had brought with them. "Was he a human?"

"Better," Tabitha said. "*So* much better. But I'll get there. Let me set the scene for you…"

"I see two Skaines," Tabitha told Katsu and Hirotoshi.

Hirotoshi nodded. The two Skaines sat in a booth on one side, deep in conversation, one making grandiloquent gestures as they conversed.

"He's gay," Tabitha pointed out.

Hirotoshi eyed her from the side. "What makes you so sure of your pronouncement? Are you even sure Skaines have an equivalent in their culture and relationships?"

"Oh, come 'on!" She turned to Hirotoshi, jerking her eyes toward the Skaines. "Have you never been around flamboyance? You can't think… Are you telling me my gaydar is all fucked up?"

"I'm merely asking," he looked at the two Skaines, "if perhaps you read too much into the situation."

"I've got good gut feelings."

Ryu snorted.

Tabitha leaned over. "I didn't ask you for your opinion."

The other guys snorted, and she glared at all of them. "You backstabbing fuckers."

This time, everyone including Tabitha chuckled. She returned to covertly paying attention to the Skaines.

One of them was wearing the soft, well-worn jumpsuit of a station employee, and the other was wearing something that likely went under a spacesuit.

Neither was armed, but Tabitha's eyes still narrowed. "I bet they're just planning their next crime spree. What planet should they go steal from? Which aliens make the best slaves?" She glared. "In fact, I'm going to go over there as soon as I finish my drink."

"Kemosabe," Hirotoshi reported, having listened to the conversation, "the one making all the gestures is talking about his mother's cooking."

"Cooking means creating a new crime. I know *all* about this stuff." Tabitha tapped her head and took another gulp. "Just as soon as I finish my drink.

"He's describing a chicken dish," Hirotoshi insisted.

"Ha! Skaines don't have chickens. Do you believe me now?"

"I was just using familiar words. It's a bird of some sort, roughly the same size as a chicken if I'm interpreting the gestures correctly."

"That's probably a code for something," Tabitha retorted snidely. "He's describing the size of something he wants to steal. Or kill. Or something." She hiccupped. "Maybe the size of his member."

"The chicken is…" Hirotoshi tilted his head, picking up the audio with his special implants, "stuffed with root vegetables and onions."

Her eyes got bigger. "Maybe they're smuggling stuff!"

Hirotoshi gave her a look. "It's a recipe. And it's spiced with something like… I don't know enough about Skaine spices to tell you."

"A bird *stuffed* with something and then *spiced* with something. Clearly, they're smuggling spiked drugs." Tabitha sat back and gave him a meaningful glance as she downed her drink and held the glass up again. "I'm done with my drink, so I'm going to go fight them. You're both falling behind, by the way."

"*You* wanted to get drunk. I'm not in a drinking contest." Katsu shook his head. "I gave up on that pursuit centuries ago."

"Good call." Tabitha rapped the table with her knuckles. "Stay sharp. We're about to have a fight."

"Kemosabe, I really think they're talking about cooking," Hirotoshi interjected. "Besides, didn't we come here to find Don Guido? We already messed up one exchange with an information broker by having a bar fight."

"How did we mess that up? We got all the information. For free. And he didn't die, so *he* can hardly complain."

"I think we should ask around and see if anyone knows Don Guido," Hirotoshi suggested.

I'm looking, Achronyx told them. *I'm plugged into the station and searching for any spelling I can think of for that name. Looking at all the ships, too.*

Anything we should know about? What about any Skaine ships? There are two shady characters in the bar right now. Tabitha accepted her fifth drink from the waitress and started sipping it immediately.

I have no ships registered to Skaines, but there is one with a Skaine crew member. It delivers medical supplies.

Hmmm. Tabitha considered this, frowning.

Just then a huge alien wearing very fancy clothing swept into the bar. Two more aliens, huge on their own but dwarfed by him, both wearing suits and carrying guns like bodyguards would, came in behind him, along with a few others in his retinue.

Tabitha and the Tontos looked at one another meaningfully.

"Bingo," Tabitha murmured quietly.

If anyone here was "Don Guido," it had to be *this* alien.

CHAPTER 12 NICKIE

Rebus Quadrant, Aboard the *Penitent Granddaughter*

Nickie tumbled into the command chair only to fidget for a minute before getting back to her feet to pace across the bridge like a feral cat. "I figure we can pose as the ship that's supposed to show up to transport the slaves. We can collect whatever part of the payment they were supposed to get on arrival, then instead of rounding up the slaves we turn them on the Skaines holding them." She folded her arms over her chest and nodded once decisively. "It'll be a cakewalk."

"I find your confidence slightly alarming." Grim sighed, though he didn't protest the idea. "It's like saying 'what could possibly go wrong?' right before you put in for retirement."

Rather than offer him some sort of reply, Nickie instead asked, "Meredith! What can you tell me about the situation we're heading toward?"

"My intel suggests there are at most five hundred

colonists," Meredith replied, taking the cue from Nickie and speaking out loud. "The colony is called 'Themis,' and is operating at level-two terraforming."

"A mining colony, then," Nickie mused, cocking her head to one side as she pondered what that would involve. "Well, at least that means it will have an atmosphere."

"That seems the most likely situation, yes," Meredith confirmed. "I feel compelled to point out that there are very few species that can survive without a breathable atmosphere, so that seems to be a rather unlikely concern regardless."

Ignoring the statement, Nickie stretched her arms over her head and once again fell back into her chair. Staying still for a few minutes was something *other* people did. "What sort of trouble should we expect?"

A report centered itself in her vision for her to glance over.

Meredith continued talking. "There is only a small contingent of Skaines guarding the colonists. I suspect they aren't expecting much trouble while they wait for transport."

Nickie shifted sideways in her chair, flinging her legs over one armrest. "Any other ships in the area?"

"Not yet," Meredith answered. "And unless the situation changes, there aren't any others due to show up until roughly two hours after our likely arrival."

Nickie let her head loll back, humming thoughtfully as she stared at the ceiling. "I guess this means we'll seriously need to have our shit together," she observed eventually. "We'll need to get the colony cleared of Skaines before backup appears."

She sat back up, letting her feet land on the floor again, and leaning over to fold her forearms on her knees. "Get in touch with the colony without alerting any of the Skaines. We need the Skaines to believe we're the transport they're expecting, but we don't want the colonists trying to fight us."

"Understood," Meredith agreed. "I'll get started."

"And see what you can find about their numbers," Nickie added hastily. "The Skaines, I mean. Their shifts and where they're stationed, too. And ideally what frequency they're communicating on."

"Leave it to me," Meredith assured her.

The data feed scrolled past the edge of Nickie's vision as she began scanning possible avenues of communication, but she ignored it for the time being. Instead, she turned her attention to Grim, who had been conspicuously silent throughout the entire exchange. He was watching her thoughtfully.

"Anything to add?" Nickie asked pointedly, leaning back in her chair and crossing one knee over the other. She stretched the top leg out to point at him with her toes. "You've been very quiet. I expected more complaining."

Grim rolled his eyes. "Your plan seems solid enough, even if I still think trying something like this with hardly any crew is crazy," he replied, shrugging one shoulder. "I'll go along with it. Besides, I'm a chef. I doubt I'll have much to do with all this."

Nickie grinned and clapped him on the shoulder. "Ah, come on, Grimkins. You know I wouldn't let you miss out on *all* the fun!"

His mandibles pulled tight to his mouth in irritation. "Why, thank you, Nick-Knack."

For a second Nickie looked almost comically offended by the absurd nickname, but then she huffed out a reluctant laugh and shrugged. "Fair play." She sighed. "Fine, fine. I'll stick with just Grim." She hopped to her feet once again and leveled the tip of one finger at him. "I'm going to go get ready for whatever's waiting for us. You should do the same. Expect the unexpected, blah blah blah. You get it."

That said, she turned on her heels and swanned off the bridge. They *were* on a battleship, after all. She had to assume there were some very fun toys that would come in handy stashed away in the nooks and crannies.

Rebus Quadrant, Skaine Ship *Boh'Locks 881*

Captain Karvar paced across the bridge. Every so often he glanced at the viewing screen, but there was never much to see in space after a ship got a certain distance from a port or a planet.

"A little over two hours until we reach our destination," the pilot reported without needing to be asked. The question had come up four times over the last hour.

Karvar sighed and finally stopped pacing, to instead sag back into the command chair. "We should be making better time than this," he groused. "We're supposed to be professionals."

"We're not making *bad* time," his first officer pointed out, glancing up from his station. "It could certainly be going worse."

"I really doubt the prospective buyers on Corona Darth are going to be quite so understanding about it," Karvar replied dryly. "The station isn't exactly known for being filled with warm and fuzzy people."

"Then the database should reject jobs that necessitate trekking into the boonies," the first officer argued, shrugging loosely.

"Especially for such a simple thing," Karvar grumbled in agreement. "Show up. Grab slaves. Leave again. Make it back to the trading port. We're going nearly a full day out of our way for a job that will take half an hour."

"But think of the money." His first officer made a show of swooning.

Karvar rolled his eyes and punched the officer's shoulder. "Sit back up before I get the smelling salts."

"It *is* a good price, though," the officer continued, dutifully sitting back up. "And once we have them, we'll be back in the Romulus Quadrant in no time."

The pilot grumbled to himself from his station, but he didn't add anything to the conversation.

"Your optimism makes me nauseous," Karvar informed his first officer blandly. "Stop it."

"I'll pass," the officer replied easily. He opened his mouth and took a deep breath, presumably to say something melodramatic and designed to get on Karvar's nerves.

Karvar held up a hand to halt him, then waved him toward the door with an air of resignation. "Spare us all and go finalize the payment for this. We're still in range of the last signal relay for the moment, and I would hate to get there just to realize that there was a complication."

His first officer snorted but got to his feet and headed

for the door. "As you command, Captain," he offered before the door slid closed behind him.

Karvar watched the door for a moment just to make sure he was gone before turning his attention back to the viewing screen. He might as well enjoy the temporary peace and quiet.

Rebus Quadrant, Themis Colony

Radio static filled the air.

It seemed like all that ever filtered through the speakers was radio static. The corresponding monitor was always blank. Raynard knew he wasn't working with the best or the newest radio tech. It had all been salvaged from older equipment, and he was pretty sure some of it was actually older than him, all to make sure the Skaines didn't pay attention to it. But it seemed unbelievable that *no one* was getting their signal.

Or maybe he just wasn't getting any sort of *return* signal. It wouldn't surprise him if the walls of the room were too thick for a signal to penetrate. It had been built to withstand a mineshaft collapsing, after all.

"Raynard?" Adelaide called from the doorway. "Come on. You've been in here all day." She stepped into the room to stand behind his chair, her hands settling on his shoulders. "At least come eat dinner. We don't need you passing out in here again."

"I still haven't heard back from Cruise," Raynard muttered rather than offering an actual reply. "It's been weeks."

"Raynard—"

"I mean, we would have seen some sign if he had been

shot down," he continued, reasoning with himself more than he was speaking to Adelaide.

"That's not necessarily true, and you know it," Adelaide interjected before he could get on another tangent. "Now come to dinner. Your equipment isn't going anywhere, and it will still be right here after you—"

A sharp tone abruptly filled the room, and Adelaide stopped talking so quickly that her teeth clicked together when she closed her mouth. Raynard scrambled for the radio, pulling the monitor closer and adjusting the settings until he could see text on the screen.

Message Received:
Is anyone on this frequency?

As Raynard began typing, Adelaide turned and bolted from the room. Raynard hardly even heard the clatter of her shoes as she sprinted, all his attention focused on the radio setup in front of him. He yanked the keyboard closer so quickly it nearly unplugged itself, and he kicked the plug back into place with the toe of one foot before he started typing.

Message Sent:
This is Mining Outpost Tykis on Themis. How can we be of assistance?

As much as he wanted to start asking for help immediately, he knew it could backfire. It was best to simply wait and play dumb at first, until he could be sure that whoever he was speaking with wasn't going to get anyone in even worse trouble.

The next message appeared almost instantaneously, too quickly for anyone to have manually typed it.

Message Received:
My intel indicates that the Skaines are not moni-
toring this frequency so I will speak freely. You
may call me Meredith. We—that is, my compan-
ions and I—are aware of the invasion, and we
wish to help. Please give me an indication of your
current status.

Raynard sagged back in his chair, its uneven legs wobbling as his weight shifted. For a moment, he was positive he was going to burst into tears. But no, he didn't have time for anything like that. He cracked his knuckles and reached for the keyboard again.

Message Sent:
Stable for now, but it won't stay that way for long.
No deaths since the initial invasion, but we had to
set up an impromptu infirmary. The Skaines
won't kill us or maim us, but they aren't shy
about putting us in our places if they think we're
getting too rowdy.

Message Received:
This isn't surprising, unfortunately. My compan-
ions and I are on a hijacked Skaine ship. We will
be breaking atmosphere within the hour under

the guise of picking all of you up for transport. It would be best if you spread this information around so that none of the colonists try to attack us when we arrive. Our purpose is to help you, so if we are forced to injure anyone due to a miscommunication, it would be counterproductive.

Message Sent:
Understood. The colony leader is on the way as we speak. He'll be caught up on everything soon, and he can explain everything to the rest of the colony. Is there anything we should do to prepare?

Message Received:
Just take precautions not to let any of the Skaines on the colony know what's going to happen. Be prepared for a lot to start happening very quickly. We can't entirely predict what will happen once we arrive, but it may not be pretty.

Message Sent:
Should we arm ourselves? I mean, we've always been a fairly docile colony, but we have a militia and some basic firearms.

Message Received:
It would be a good precaution, but I would advise against trying to start anything. We can handle ourselves. If any of you try to help it will likely

result in you getting in the way at best, or getting yourself or someone else killed at worst. We're professionals. We know what we're doing.

He wanted to ask what kind of professionals they were, but he knew he was running out of time before he would need to leave the room. And if he were honest, he didn't much care what sort of professionals they were, as long as they could actually get the Skaines off the colony.

Raynard glanced over his shoulder in time to see Adelaide lead Keen into the room when he heard two pairs of footsteps rapidly approaching.

"What's the situation?" Keen asked, leaning over Raynard's shoulder.

Raynard leaned to the side and turned the monitor to let Keen read it himself rather than rehashing the entire conversation.

Keen was silent as he read it, and silent afterward as he let it sink in. Then he took a deep breath and sighed it out. "Adelaide?"

"Keen?"

"I need to meet with everyone after dinner," he stated, voice level. "Can you make sure the message gets around? I will explain everything to everyone then."

Adelaide nodded rapidly. "Of course, sir. In the emergency shelter again?"

"That would be best, yes," he agreed, before stepping from Raynard's chair and quickly beginning to make his way out of the room.

Raynard and Adelaide were both quiet for a moment, staring at the text on the monitor as if they were both waiting for it to disappear. It was as if they were both expecting it to be an elaborate hallucination and realize they were still in the exact same mess they had been in.

When the text remained on the screen, though, Adelaide laughed suddenly, clapping her hands over her mouth at the last second. Beside her, Raynard was grinning at the monitor. He got to his feet and tugged Adelaide closer, kissing her swiftly before he lifted her off the ground and twirled her in a joyous circle.

They were being rescued!

Laughing still, she swatted his shoulder. She waited until her feet were back on the ground before she caught his hand and tugged him out of the room. If she was going to spread a message during dinner, she needed to actually be at dinner.

Rebus Quadrant, Themis Colony, Mess Hall

Dinner was a strange but quiet affair that evening. It was hard to relax and have a conversation with a dozen Skaines patrolling the tables. Even so, there was a thrum of energy in the air, like a live wire waiting to spark.

Adelaide tapped the end of her fork against the side of her still-half-full tray. The movement seemed absent-minded to anyone who didn't know the significance.

Only a few people glanced at her, but she knew that she had the entire room's attention. She tapped her fork against the tray four more times, leaning her chin in her other hand and staring into the middle distance. She looked listless and tired; as harmless and as innocent as a lamb.

"Quit that racket," one of the guards snapped. "Otherwise you can finish your meal with your hands." A surprisingly gentle threat, considering it wasn't unheard of for them to simply take meals away when they were annoyed. It wasn't the sort of thing she was inclined to question just then, though.

Adelaide glanced at him over her shoulder, but she didn't reply. They all knew that none of the Skaines ever wanted them to actually talk, and it was just easier in the long run not to—especially when they couldn't risk too much attention just then.

She ate a few more bites before she set her fork down, instead drumming her fingers on the tabletop. Four times, then two times, then three, and then four again. To all appearances, she was simply bored and waiting for an unsatisfactory meal to end. She could practically feel the guard scowling at the back of her head, but there was nothing he could do. He couldn't exactly take her *hand* from her. That would be property damage, and then he would have to pay for her.

Not exactly a warm and fuzzy thought, but that was what was keeping her safe just then, and she wasn't going to look a gift horse in the mouth.

It was a simple code, thought up in a hurry when the Skaines had first invaded and based on the tapping code designed for when a shaft collapsed and trapped someone in the mine. It just let everyone know when Keen needed to see them all. After all, it was easy to lose track of their jailers in the deeper reaches of the outpost. No one knew the mines and the outpost better than the colonists.

Adelaide fought back a smile. If the Skaines noticed, they would figure out that something was up. A slave's duty was not to be happy, after all. So she slumped loosely in her seat, gaze distant and unfocused as she watched the wall across the room, even though her heart was pounding a mile a minute in her chest and she wanted to leap out of her seat.

CHAPTER 13 TABITHA

Farha Station, Yeven's Bar

"That is definitely him," Tabitha insisted. She looked at Hirotoshi and Katsu. "Bet?"

"As I recall," Hirotoshi reminded her smoothly, "there was a bet last time about who could punch the most people in a bar fight, and neither you nor Ryu paid up."

"I will this time! What are we betting? Push-ups? Five hundred push-ups."

"Since you didn't pay up last time, make it a thousand." Hirotoshi smiled at her and sipped his drink, looking down at the liquid. "This really is much better than the other stuff."

"What other stuff?" Katsu asked.

"We can get you one," Tabitha offered.

Hirotoshi shook his head slightly, hinting strongly to Katsu not to agree.

"You ruin all my fun." Tabitha stuck her tongue out at him. "All right, how about this? Since I didn't pay up last time, not *only* will we make it a thousand push-ups, I'll put my bet on 'no.'"

"I think we can take that bet," Katsu joked.

"Hell, I probably need to work out." Tabitha gave them a big grin and downed her last drink. "All right, let's go see."

Hirotoshi and Katsu picked up their drinks and drifted after her as she made her way through the bar, weaving slightly. By the time she reached the other side of the room, however, her head was completely clear.

She shook her head over her shoulder at the guys. "All that work and the buzz already wore off," she groused. "I tell ya, I'm an expensive date."

Katsu chuckled. "It would be, as Bobcat would say, funny as hell to watch some desperate guy trying to pour drinks down you, though."

She looked at him, nonplussed. "I'm not going out with any guy unless I've already decided he gets a chance to ride the rollercoaster." Tabitha smacked her ass with a grin, and punched Hirotoshi in the shoulder when he gave her a pained look at the euphemism. "Oh, come on, Number One, that was a good one."

Hirotoshi took a sip of his drink, trying to ignore the situation as much as possible.

Tabitha laughed and pointed at the massive blue alien. Next to him was a thinner alien, slightly shorter than a normal human and green. The two bodyguards were brownish, and their skin almost looked like they were made of rocks.

"So Katsu bets that Big Blue is Don Guido?" Tabitha looked at the two of them for nods of agreement, then slipped around the entourage to hop up on a table and tap the huge alien on the shoulder. "Hey, Big Blue, what's your name?"

"Oh, *dear*," Hirotoshi murmured, looking around to identify who he needed to worry about.

The blue alien shook off Tabitha's hand. "Get lost," he muttered. His voice sounded like gravel. His two bodyguards jumped up and frowned at Tabitha.

"Hey, now." Tabitha grinned down at the alien. "No reason to get grumpy just because someone's taller than you for a few minutes."

"I said, get lost." The alien shook his head at her.

"This could still go well," Katsu soothed Hirotoshi.

Tabitha's face darkened. "I just want to know your fucking name, jackoff!"

"I stand here, *in person, unfortunately*, corrected," Katsu muttered.

The alien jerked his head at the bodyguards. "Get her out of my face."

Tabitha stood up, one arm on her hip and the other pointing at him. "Oh, hell no, you jerk! I want your fucking name!"

"All right," Katsu began. "I'll flank left, and you—" He looked around, but Hirotoshi was already gone, sliding into one of the seats vacated by a member of the entourage. Hirotoshi leaned into the skinny green alien and clinked his glass. They seemed to be holding a drinking contest. "So I'm alone on backup," Katsu grumbled. "Great." *Achronyx, anything you can give me for helpful advice here?*

Yes. Don't get into fights with several large aliens at once.

Not helpful, Achronyx!

On the contrary, given that you could still walk away, it seems to be eminently useful advice.

Katsu was going to respond, but the first alien sailed past his head.

I'll get back to you, Achronyx.

You're not going to take my advice, are you?

As one of the bodyguards tried to clamber up on the back of a couch to get to Tabitha, Katsu took a flying leap and tackled him over a table and onto the floor. They rolled, glasses and silverware clattering around them.

No, probably not.

I tried.

Tabitha, meanwhile, had avoided the first bodyguard when Katsu had tackled him, and avoided the second by leaping off the table she was standing on, and onto the back of the giant alien as he stood up to get away from the fight.

"Hey, asswipe!" She rapped the top of his skull with her knuckles. "Tell me your name, for fuck's sake!"

The alien, finding Tabitha to be heavier than expected, tried to shake her off his shoulders and also tried to bat at her, but his range of motion didn't allow him to hit her. Tabitha scrambled up to perch on his shoulders, directing a punch at his shoulder to emphasize her point.

"Why are you being such a jerk about this?" she demanded.

A loud crash caught everyone's attention, and they looked over in time to see one of the bodyguards slide down the back wall of the bar, surrounded by broken glass. There was a polite round of applause.

"See?" Tabitha slapped the blue alien. "The rest of these people are cool. Why do you have to be Dr. SuckMyAss?"

"Kemosabe, one is sneaking up behind you!" Katsu yelled.

"Ugh, I have to do *everything* myself." Tabitha directed a last punch at the blue alien and vaulted forward, flipping and landing with one leg out on the floor.

The other bodyguard, who had been hoping to knock her off his boss's head, tackled his boss instead. An angry roar filled the room as the blue alien turned around to cuff the bodyguard for his mistake.

"I hired you for one thing—so I can drink in peace—and you fail me!"

Tabitha was laughing. "Ha. This Don Guido is a taskmaster.

Wait, Achronyx said to her. *Don Guido. I have a thought. Let me check something.*

Sure. I don't have anything going on until he stops beating up his bodyguard.

There was a pause, then Achronyx reported, *"Don Guido" means "still waters rolling" in the local dialect.*

Wait. Wait, wait, wait. Tabitha looked at the huge alien. *So when I told Guildert that I would never try to intimidate someone named Guido...*

Yes. 'Waters rolling.' Like a wave.

No wonder he looked confused.

Quite.

Well, I suppose Big Blue here is water-colored.

Personally, I am not sure he is the alien you're looking for.

You and I are both on that side of the bet, then. Hey, where's Hirotoshi?

Judging by the physical data I am receiving, he is engaging in a drinking contest of some kind.

Tabitha peered around and saw that Achronyx was right. Hirotoshi and the skinny green alien were both downing shots that had been brought by the Torcellan waitress, who had managed to weave between the big blue alien and his bodyguard with the ease of long experience, not spilling a drop.

Hirotoshi and the green alien shouted simultaneously and shook their heads to clear them. Whatever was in the shots must be strong.

"Could you *help* a bit?" Tabitha called.

"I'm making contacts," Hirotoshi called back raising his glass to her, unperturbed.

"Ugh." Tabitha looked up as the blue alien turned around to glare at her. "*Finally.* We were having a conversation. It was rude to interrupt."

The blue alien stomped over to her and bent down to glare into her face. "We weren't having a conversation. *You* were annoying me. Buzz off."

Tabitha punched him in the face and yelled, "Hell no! I'm not just going to buzz off. I want to know your damned *name.*"

He reached out to pick her up, drawing his other hand back to punch her across the room, but Tabitha was already gone. She clambered up his body again to straddle his neck and punched his head over and over.

"Tell. Me. Your. Fucking. *Name!*"

"Get off me!" The alien staggered around, pulling at her legs.

She was clearly stronger than he expected, and Tabitha

snickered at him.

"Not as weak as you thought, huh, Big Blue?" She patted a leg. "Let me tell you, I'm like a Black Widow. If I want my guy to stay put, he's going to stay put!"

"Stop calling me that name!" He directed a punch at her and she leaned her torso back to get out of the way, coming face to face with one of the bodyguards. Judging by the bruises and the many cuts in his clothing, this was the one who'd met the bar mirror at high speed.

"Hey, ugly." Tabitha, still hanging backward and upside-down, punched him and managed to get him on the bottom of the jaw.

He tried to pull her off the blue alien, who was yelling at him to stop. Katsu fixed the issue by tackling him again and punching him hard in the mouth. The bodyguard howled in pain.

"These things take a hit like a bear," Katsu complained. "And they hit like a truck."

I did warn you, Achronyx told both of them.

But we're having fun, Tabitha argued. She flipped herself upright and grabbed one of the rafters, swinging away just as the blue alien managed to start prying her legs away from his neck. "Hey, Big Blue, over here!"

He growled and charged her, and she swung her feet up to catch him square in the chest. With his speed and mass, the hit stopped them *both* cold and jolted all the way up to Tabitha's hands.

She dropped to the floor with a curse, waving her hands. "Son of a ball-sucking titty-fucker, that *hurt*!" When she looked up, Hirotoshi and the green alien clinked glasses, poured a shot glass into a taller glass full of liquid, and downed the whole thing. "Number One! What the fuck are you doing?"

Hirotoshi was too busy drinking to respond.

"Bastard," Tabitha muttered, looking around.

Another member of the alien's entourage stepped into the fight. Delicate, with pale-pink skin, the alien swept aside long sleeves and tipped its hands out, palms up. Its fingers closed around something that at first looked like thin air...

And then long blades extended out in segments to turn into a glass-like weapon that looked razor-sharp and spiky all over.

"Fucknuggets!" Tabitha scrabbled out of the way as the delicate alien came at her in a rush. *This thing is fucking fast! What are those, Achronyx?*

They appear to be some sort of glass that can be changed in shape and hardness, but I am not certain how it is controlled. If you could perhaps steal it—

I'll work on that, sure! Tabitha dodged again, and her eyes widened as one of the knives embedded itself inches deep in the floor. *Motherfucker! Did you see that?*

I assume your question was rhetorical. Also, is this really the time for conversation?

Tabitha lashed out with one arm rather than answer. She hit the delicate alien before the thing could pull its weapon free of the floor, and was gratified to hear it shriek in pain.

"So you *do* have a weakness!" Tabitha kicked out to shove it away and grabbed the handle of the glass thing.

To her annoyance, it melted into a puddle.

"Aw, man, I wanted to try that!" She didn't waste time

on it, though. She went on the offense with a vengeance, rushing the other alien and planting her foot in its chest to give a sharp shove.

It somersaulted backward over a table and landed on its face on the floor. Though it was still moving faintly, it didn't seem inclined to get up and rejoin the fight.

"That's sorted." Tabitha dusted her hands.

Big hands seized her and dragged her backward by her hair.

"Ow! Sonofabitch! What are you doing?" She crab-walked backward. "Let go!"

"Get out of this bar!" the blue alien yelled at her. He threw her into the courtyard and bared his teeth. "Get *lost*, puny alien."

Tabitha, who had hopped back to her feet, looked at him with glowing red eyes and elongated teeth.

Her voice dropped a notch. "*That* was a mistake, fuck-tard. You *never* mess with a Hispanic woman's hair."

The alien froze, staring at her new face with trepidation.

Tabitha reached for her lapels and took her coat off, setting it to the side and cracking her knuckles. "Yeah, you fucked up, Big Blue. So I'll ask you one. More. Time. What's your *name*?"

He had the sense not to run from her, at least. He put his head down and charged.

Tabitha waited until the last second to duck under his arms and step aside, and he tumbled headlong into an ornamental fountain. It exploded, showering both of them in chemically-treated water that smelled of algae and fake floral scent.

"Yech!" Tabitha brushed water out of her eyes, then walked into the puddle and hauled the alien out by his soggy robes. "Come on, fucker, fight's not over yet."

He swung at her, and she dodged. The floor was slippery, but her boots were the very best technology the Etheric Empire had come up with, and she kept her footing as she leaned back and landed a roundhouse kick on the alien's face, while keeping her head and torso well below the level he was punching at.

He clutched his face and howled.

"Fine! I don't know why you even care, but my name is Klio!"

Tabitha stopped and stared at him. "*Klio?*"

He wiped water off his face and glared at her. "Yeah. Klio. *Now* will you stop calling me 'Big Blue' and let me have a drink? What kind of aliens are you, anyway?" He stomped back toward the bar, still muttering.

"Kemosabe." Katsu appeared at her shoulder, covered in spilled alcohol and alien blood. He looked at her. "You look terrible. You smell terrible, too."

She frowned at him. "Rude, Katsu. You should never tell a woman she smells."

"All right. Oh jewel of femininity, I would not recommend this present fragrance as your regular perfume."

Tabitha snickered and grabbed her coat. "Okay. Come on, let's go rescue Hirotoshi."

They walked back into the bar, where the bartender gave them a glare. Tabitha sauntered up to the bar and assured him that she knew what was what on this station, sending a sizable transfer of cash from Achronyx. The money solved all problems, and the bartender welcomed them once more with a smile and a fresh round of drinks.

"That was easy," Tabitha told the Tonto. "You know, I like this place. You start a bar fight, you pay for a round of drinks, everyone's cool."

"It's quite civilized," Katsu agreed.

Achronyx weighed in with, *You two are barbarians.*

Seriously, Achronyx? Do I have to teach everyone manners today? Tabitha shook her head and looked around before pointing. "There's Hirotoshi. God, are they still drinking?"

The two of them headed over to the entourage's table. The bodyguards and Klio looked up at them warily, but Tabitha pointedly ignored them and raised an eyebrow at Hirotoshi and his companion.

"Oh, Tabitha." Hirotoshi looked up and gestured to the thin green alien beside him. "I'm glad you're back. I would like to introduce you to this fine gentleman. *This* is Don Guido."

CHAPTER 14 NICKIE

Rebus Quadrant, Themis Colony, Aboard the *Penitent Granddaughter*

Entering atmosphere. Landing in T-minus thirty seconds. I'm in contact with the Skaines in charge, and so far they believe we're a Skaine ship. The money has been transferred.

Meredith was no-nonsense as she made the announcement. Nickie quickly checked her equipment one last time as she headed for the airlock. Meredith continued updating her on the situation as she walked.

The ruse will likely end as soon as you step off of the ship and they see you are not a Skaine. Once that happens, I will lock down the ship's systems to keep any hacking attempts at bay.

And to keep them from getting back the money, Nickie added.

That is not my primary concern at this time, but that will be one side effect of locking down the systems, yes.

Grim was already standing at the airlock when Nickie got there, shifting back and forth on his feet.

"You sure this is going to work out?" he wondered, stepping out of the way as Nickie opened the inner doors to the airlock. "Still seems kind of reckless, if you ask me." His eyes narrowed slightly as he added, "Besides, you were drinking. I really doubt that's going to help the situation, and I have to figure that even Meredith can only do so much."

Nickie clicked her tongue. "Well, yeah, no shit," she agreed before she lifted a hand to point at her chest with her thumb. "And that's where *I* take over." She offered him a grin and a sarcastic salute before she stepped into the airlock. "You worry too much," she assured him. "Now get back to the bridge so you can enjoy the show."

Grim scowled at her for a moment, unconvinced, but he stepped back to let the airlock doors close all the same.

Nickie rolled her shoulders, flexed her hands, cracked her neck and back, and bounced in place on the balls of her feet. By the time the airlock's outer doors opened and the ramp extended, she was loose and ready for anything.

With an easy sway to her hips, she sauntered down the ramp to the airfield.

Already, she could see a few of the Skaines making their way out of the outpost, heading to the airfield to see what was going on—and to see why a human was disembarking from a Skaine ship, evidently of her own free will. By the time Nickie was at the base of the ramp, the number of Skaines coming to investigate had doubled.

Nickie didn't give them a chance to think about it for long before she unholstered her gun and started firing. Two of the Skaines dropped like sacks of rocks before the rest of them burst into a flurry of activity, diving for cover and reaching for their own weapons.

She launched into a cartwheel as she dodged the first round of fire. When her boots hit the ground again and she straightened back up, she was beside one of the handful of fuel stockpiles. She eyed the barrels contemplatively for a second and backed up a few paces.

Nickie broke into a sprint, practically flying at one of the enormous industrial fuel drums until she leapt and slammed into it with the force of a battering ram. The stack of barrels collapsed and Nickie pirouetted out of the way. When she came to a standstill again, she watched one of the barrels roll right into the path of the Skaines' laser fire. She dove out of the way and covered her head as the barrel exploded.

Cautiously, she peered up again, to see that half of the Skaines had been sent flying with the explosion. When she had gotten back to her feet, it took her a moment to realize that the hem of one of her pant legs had caught on fire. She patted the fire out before it had a chance to take hold.

Advanced healing is in effect, but please try not to turn yourself into a torch.

I like to live life on the edge.

The remaining Skaines were already recovering from the explosion, and Nickie rolled her shoulders to loosen up so she could launch into a handspring when one of them charged at her. She pivoted on one foot when she landed, planting her other foot in the middle of the Skaine's back to kick him straight into another Skaine. They stumbled into oncoming fire. Both of them landed in a heap after they were riddled with holes.

She was close to the outpost by then, and there were scarcely any of the first wave of Skaines left. Nickie grinned to herself, and some of the Skaines slowed when they saw it. They were having second thoughts, but she didn't plan on giving them any time to act on them.

Gun raised, she shot the nearest Skaine three times. She twisted out of the way of another laser blast, only to accidentally crash into a Skaine behind her. She huffed out an indignant breath, slammed her elbow into his chin, and turned in a circle, stretching a leg out to sweep his feet out from under him.

His throat made a fascinating cracking noise under her boot. She lifted the body off of the ground and threw it toward the remaining Skaines. They scattered and the body landed on the ground without incident, but it did distract them enough for her to pick the last of them off with her gun, one after the other, with rapid-fire precision.

For a moment after that, everything was quiet. It was a strangely dissonant sort of serenity.

Nickie looked at the bodies surrounding her, head cocked to one side. "That was quick," she remarked to herself, planting her hands on her hips. She kept walking, stepping over bodies as she did.

Hey, Meredith?

She peered carefully around the edge of the doorway as she got to the main entrance of the outpost.

Tell the colonists to be ready for anything, but to stand down. I'm doing a sweep of the outpost, and I don't need some chuckle-fuck with delusions of grandeur getting in my way.

I will pass the message along. Do you need anything else, or are you content to continue murdering your way through the outpost?

"Hi ho, hi ho, it's off to work I go," Nickie recited aloud, twirling one finger in the air in time with the words. "You just keep me abreast of the situation, yeah? If anyone so much as takes a shit, I want to be on top of it." She paused for a moment when she realized how that sounded and shook her head briefly. "You know what I mean."

Of course. Good luck.

Nickie scoffed. "Seriously? I don't need luck. I have ammo." She broke into a jog through the main hall, heading deeper into the outpost.

Rebus Quadrant, Themis Colony

An explosion rattled the room, and the colonists jolted in surprise. Some of them shrieked, and others dove for cover. A chilly calm settled over the lot of them and Keen wondered mostly to himself, "What in the world are they getting up to out there?"

Rather than a response, his communicator went off. When he answered it, bemused, an unfamiliar voice spoke to him.

"Keen. This is Meredith. I've been instructed to tell all of you to bunker down somewhere safe. Things at the airfield have gotten a bit more eventful than we initially anticipated."

"Understood," Keen agreed. She disconnected without another word, leaving him blinking at his communicator for a moment before he put it away.

"Was that one of them?" Adelaide wondered, standing at his side. Keen simply nodded once in reply.

"They want us to get into hiding for the time being," he added after a moment. His tone turned dry. "Apparently things are getting a bit heated outside."

"How do we know we can even trust them?" Adelaide asked, her voice low as she moved closer to Keen. "All we have so far are messages on a screen and some explosions at the airfield. We don't know anything about them."

Keen sighed, stressed and tired. He dragged a hand down his face. "At the moment, we might as well. If it turns out they aren't actually here to help we'll fight back, but I'm not going to start throwing people into combat before I know it's necessary."

Adelaide nodded slowly, and Keen clapped her on the shoulder. "In the meantime, we all need to get down into the mines and scatter. I don't know if the Skaines are going to come looking for us while all of that," he gestured in the general direction of the explosion, "is still going on, but I would rather they not find all of us all at once if they are."

He looked around briefly until he spotted a chair. He climbed onto it and whistled sharply, and all eyes in the room snapped to him.

"We're going to break off into groups and scatter into the mines for the time being," he explained. "Make sure each group has at least one militia member, and try not to hide in the same place as another group once you're down there. I'll let everyone know once the coast is clear and then we'll all congregate in the main hall. Does everyone understand?"

Sounds of agreements rang out and Keen hopped down from the chair to begin making rounds through the room, overseeing things as everyone separated into groups. Remarkably quickly, they began vacating the room.

Nothing could ever go perfectly seamlessly, though. When one of the groups heard a few Skaines in the halls, Adelaide and Raynard volunteered to distract them and lure them away.

Shouting and jeering, they distracted the Skaines and then sprinted into the halls, luring the trio of Skaines away from the rest of their group. They ran until they turned into a hallway, then ducked into a closet. They closed the door as silently as they could, kept the lights off, and huddled together at the back of the closet until they heard the Skaines pass.

They waited until the coast was clear before Raynard turned on the lights. By that point, it would be safer if they just stayed where they were rather than trying to catch up with the others. They took a moment to look around the closet, finding mostly cleaning supplies and a few half-full filing cabinets, but also some of the militia's backup weapons.

Cautiously, they both picked up a gun.

Adelaide turned the gun in her hands this way and that way, inspecting it closely. She had never held a weapon before—she hadn't been part of the colony's minuscule militia—but it seemed pretty straightforward.

"I mean, we might be able to help?" she ventured. "A little bit, at least. This doesn't look *so* complicated. Just… point, pull, repeat."

"Point, pull, repeat," Raynard agreed, a virtually identical gun in his hands. He gazed at her for a moment with what Adelaide assumed must be deep affection. She placed a hand on his.

"Not quite what I had in mind when I left home." He sighed, leaning over to put the gun down on the nearest shelf.

"Hey." His fingers closed around Adelaide's gun and gently pulled it out of her grasp to set it down with his. "Before this gets any further—"

He didn't get a chance to say anything else before Adelaide surged toward him, gripping the front of his shirt in two white-knuckled fists as their mouths crashed together. Their hands began to wander, and it seemed almost inevitable when their clothing began to land on the floor.

The main hall was empty as Nickie jogged through it. She pulled her drones from her belt pouch and tossed them into the air, and the metallic orbs zipped off in separate directions. Nickie used it as a chance to catch her breath, paying half-hearted attention to their video feeds in the corner of her vision.

It took a few moments, but by the time her drones had finished scoping out the site she had a loose idea of how the rest of the Skaines were scattered throughout the outpost. She didn't bother to recall the drones immediately, letting them continue to whizz through the outpost. Every so often a Skaine on the video feed dropped to the ground in a puddle of blood and viscera as the drones ripped through them like a knife through cheese.

They were handy toys, but Nickie wasn't going to let them do all the work for her. She took off at a sprint down the nearest hallway.

She came to the first group of Skaines sorting through a stockpile of weapons. They whipped around to face her when she fired her gun once. Well, all but one of them turned to face her, as the one she shot fell face-forward onto the floor, his gun clattering away.

In an instant they were firing on her, laser light reflecting off the walls. Nickie dropped to the floor and tumbled to the side. She fired again and a second Skaine dropped to the floor, which opened up enough of a space for her to hop back to her feet without getting shot. She fired three more times, hitting two more Skaines and the corner of the wall, leaving just two Skaines standing.

They cast about wildly for some sort of cover, but there was nothing but the wall and the weapons behind them, and nothing ahead of them but Nickie.

You're beginning to draw attention from other Skaines still in the outpost.

Good. Means I don't need to go looking for them.

She dropped into a backbend to avoid a shot, and by then she was close enough to simply kick one of the Skaines in the chin as she launched herself into a back handspring. His head snapped back with a crunch, and he crumpled to the ground.

She heard more of them approaching. Quickly she coiled herself at the hips and launched a roundhouse kick, knocking the last Skaine's gun from his hand and sending him stumbling to the side. Once disarmed, it was easy to shoot him in the chest, and then she didn't need to worry about them closing in on her from both sides.

Just in time, as another group rounded the corner, ready for a fight.

I have an update.

Make it quick. Nickie ducked beneath a shot. It went wide and clipped a wall, sending a shower of concrete gravel to the floor. She scooped a handful of it up.

Thermal scans indicate that two of the colonists have locked themselves in a weapons closet. Their core body temperatures are rising rapidly.

Meredith said nothing else after that and Nickie threw her handful of dust into the nearest Skaine's face. As he recoiled, coughing and scrubbing at his eyes, Nickie kicked him in the chest and sent him sprawling to the ground.

Okay? she asked eventually, planting one heel on the downed Skaine's chest. *I'm not sure what I'm supposed to do with that information.*

She fired a single shot between the Skaine's eyes.

I believe they're mid-coitus.

Meredith sounded remarkably casual—almost *cheerful*—as she informed Nickie of that development.

The only thing that kept Nickie from grinding to a halt was the trio of Skaines rushing her. She turned on her heels, ran three steps up the wall, and backflipped over the trio to land behind them.

Meredith.

Her voice was calm even as she shot two of the Skaines in the back and hurled her boot knife at the third.

Why the fuck do I need to know that?

She stepped toward the three bodies and pulled her knife out of the third one's skull with a soggy squelch.

Please, enlighten me.

She slid her knife back into its sheath.

There was a beat, and Nickie had a moment of horrible dread before Meredith replied.

Merely keeping you abreast of the situation as you asked.

Nickie groaned and dragged one hand down her face. As an afterthought, she held her gun out to the side and shot the Skaine who was peering around the corner in the chest.

She didn't deign to offer Meredith a reply, instead turning her attention back to the task at hand. There were eleven dead Skaines surrounding her and a whole lot more than that along her back trail, but she knew that still wasn't all of the Skaines on the colony.

She jogged back in the direction she had come from, checking the video feed to see where she should head next. She didn't like to leave a job half-finished.

She wasn't going to say it was *easy*, but it was hardly the most difficult thing she had ever done. And they were all so raring for a fight that they practically lined up to charge at her. She found them scattered throughout the outpost in groups of four and five and six, and once she found one group, there was likely to be another on the way by the time she finished with the first.

While common sense told her that considerable time had passed, it still felt like no time at all before she found herself standing in front of the last group. Six of them were barricaded in an office, upended cabinets in front of the door to block the way into the room without obscuring their lines of sight.

It wasn't a bad idea really, but Nickie was pretty sure they had forgotten who they were dealing with.

She backed up a few paces and broke into a run, twisting and weaving around laser blasts that seemed to be coming toward her in slow motion. She launched herself forward, arms stretched out as she jumped through the gap the barricade didn't cover. She slammed into one of the Skaines, using him to cushion her landing, then bounced to her feet, already twisting to kick out. She nailed a second Skaine in the chest, and he stumbled back and slid down into the wall, wheezing.

She fired once at the Skaine she had landed on to make sure he didn't get up, and then at the two to her left. Just like that, there were only three remaining.

She twisted to face one, leaning aside to avoid his shot. She caught his arm, bending his wrist to make him drop his gun, and she slammed the heel of her hand into his neck. As he was reeling, she turned her attention to the one still standing.

He was staring at her with blank, wide eyes. She suspected he had already accepted the fact that he wasn't getting away from her, and one after the other, she shot him and the two wheezing on the floor.

It took a second after that for her to realize that she was the only one still alive in that room, and she looked around slowly before heaving a relieved sigh.

Nickie doubled over, hands on her knees as she caught her breath. *Hey, Meredith. Can you tell Grim to meet me in the main hall? I think I've cleared out the Skaines occupying the outpost.*

Right away.

Nickie recalled her drones as an afterthought, and after they were secure in her belt clips she climbed over the barricade.

CHAPTER 15 TABITHA

Farha Station, Yeven's Bar

Tabitha's mouth hung open. What the fuck? *This* was Don Guido?

But now that Achronyx had told her what Don Guido actually meant, she supposed she shouldn't be so surprised. She looked at the booth. "You two should scooch. I want to get in on this drinking game."

The skinny green alien looked as though he might be sick merely at the thought, and Hirotoshi moved out of the booth hastily.

"Perhaps we should help Don Guido get some air," he suggested meaningfully.

"Right. Katsu, help Number One get Don Guido out of here." Tabitha looked around and saw the whole rest of the entourage staring at her. She nodded to Big Blue. "Klio."

She smirked as she walked out of the bar. These aliens weren't even human, and they were *still* all staring at her ass.

Even in her backup leather pants.

"Still got it," she murmured to herself. Her lips curved in a smile.

Level Fifteen, it turned out, was full of bars, and a few minutes later they managed to find a table at one of them. Hirotoshi was coaxing a glass of water into Don Guido while Katsu and Tabitha looked on in amusement from the bar.

He came over a few minutes later.

"Katsu hasn't started his push-ups yet," Tabitha reported. "So you haven't missed anything. You two can start together."

Katsu jumped and looked at her. "I'd forgotten the bet."

"Yep," Tabitha said smugly. "Double or nothing, baby."

"I cannot believe you got out of the push-ups you should have had to do for the first bar fight," Hirotoshi muttered. He shook his head and looked at the alien. "I figured I'd get in good with the entourage, and when I realized he was Don Guido, I figured I'd get in good with *him*. I think I overshot."

At the table, Don Guido clapped a hand over his mouth and only barely managed to keep from vomiting.

"Just a little," Katsu agreed, putting up two fingers a scant millimeter apart with a wink to Tabitha. "A tiny bit."

Hirotoshi sighed and got another glass of water from the bartender. "He'll be sober enough to talk soon, I promise."

"Not *too* sober," Tabitha called after him in Japanese. "We want him to be honest, remember?"

Hirotoshi held up a hand in acknowledgment and sat

back down at the table to keep nursing Don Guido back to health.

"So," Katsu suggested as she came up, "let's try every alcohol they've got."

"Deal." Tabitha hopped up on a stool and flagged down the bartender. "Two of everything, please. We're trying it all."

The bartender looked cautious. "Some of it will probably be toxic to you."

"That's the fun!" Tabitha exclaimed excitedly.

The bartender looked at her face and decided not to argue. He shuffled off with a sigh to get two of everything.

At least he would make some money from this.

A large, bipedal alien with dark fur ducked into Yeven's Bar and looked around, taking in every detail. He had already noted the broken fountain outside, which was being repaired by the little robots that kept Farha Station operational.

It and the bar would be as good as new by the dinner rush.

Inside the bar, one of the bartender's assistants was sweeping up broken glass and mopping up alcohol and blood from the floor. The broken tables and chairs had been hauled over to one side of the room for repairs.

The patrons—those who still remained in the bar—had returned to their drinks while keeping a wary eye on the door. A few clearly didn't like the look of this new alien, either.

The alien made his way to the bar and leaned on it. It creaked under his weight.

He jerked his head at the bartender. "You see what happened with the fight?"

It was a courtesy question. Bartenders always knew. You didn't keep a bar open on Farha Station without having a keen eye for patrons and their doings.

Which was exactly what Borven Thod, Interstation Inspector, needed right now.

He followed up his question by sliding his badge across the counter, making sure that it would be caught by the security cameras. He had no need for secrecy in this case, and he liked to have proof that he had come to a particular place. Inspectors didn't always have the best reputation, so it was good to leave a trail.

This bartender did not betray by so much as a flicker of expression whether he was glad to have Borven here or not. He picked up the badge and inspected it, then nodded respectfully to Borven.

"I did indeed see what happened," the bartender told him. He nodded discreetly to one of the aliens sitting at a table, surrounded by hangers-on and some bodyguards. "I suppose you could say that he started it."

Borven sighed as he looked at the inhabitants of the table. He had been tracking some particular aliens across a few space stations, now, and that blue behemoth didn't fit the description at all.

Still, he was here. He nodded for the bartender to keep talking.

"Of course, he was provoked," the bartender continued smoothly, hedging his bets so that no one could say he had thrown them under the bus. "One of the humans was very insistent on knowing his name."

"*Humans?*" Borven's head whipped around.

He had been right to stay, because he was tracking the humans. Humans with pale skin and dark hair, who carried swords and guns.

Humans who stirred up bar fights wherever they went.

"Are they still here?"

"No, they left with another alien not too long ago," the bartender answered, grabbing a bottle of green liquid that had bubbles.

Borven nodded in thanks and headed out of the bar to look around some more. He was hot on the trail, and it shouldn't take too much time to find the humans. After all, there weren't many in this sector.

Don Guido wasn't the first person Hirotoshi had nursed through a hangover, and between the water and the concoctions he discreetly poured into it, the skinny alien was able to speak coherently after a few minutes.

"How much did we *drink?*" he groaned.

Hirotoshi shrugged as if he couldn't remember. In fact, he could have listed every beverage they had drunk, but he didn't think that would make the alien feel better.

"Did you say you were an information broker?" he asked casually. Tabitha and Katsu had appeared and were drawing their chairs up to the table quietly, so as not to distract Don Guido.

Don Guido thought very hard about this with all the

effort and dignity of someone who was still very drunk. Finally, he offered, "I don't know if I told you that, but I am one."

Katsu pressed his lips together. He was trying fairly hard not to laugh.

"What luck," Hirotoshi exclaimed. He smiled at Don Guido. "We need some information. I don't suppose you'd be willing to make a deal..."

"I could make a deal." Don Guido grabbed a menu and looked it over. "You can pay my tab at the other bar."

"Done," Tabitha agreed promptly.

Don Guido turned to look at her, goggle-eyed. "Where did you come from?"

"A place of sugar and spice and everything nice. But the Neanderthal with no sense of humor next to you thinks I was born in a barn," Tabitha answered him. The joke went right over his head, but he nodded solemnly anyway. "So, here's what we're looking for—"

If I might interject, Achronyx said suddenly. *It appears an interstation inspector is looking for you three. Perhaps you should come back to the ship.*

Why is he looking for us?

Because of your penchant for starting bar fights.

I don't start the fights. She took a gulp of her drink. *I never start the fights. Ask anyone.*

Because of your penchant for being around when fights spontaneously come into being, then. He's headed your way.

We won't start any fights, and he won't have any reason to bring us in. But Tabitha leaned close to Katsu and Hirotoshi. "An interstation inspector is looking for some people who have been in bar fights recently."

"Weren't you just in a bar fight?" Don Guido piped up, looking at Hirotoshi.

"No, you're thinking of someone else." Tabitha grinned at him.

"Oh." He looked at his glass of water with wide eyes, as if trying to figure out what it was. "I suppose that's possible."

"Anyway, what we need to know is what's going on with the Skaines in this sector." Tabitha leaned in, her face intent.

"I don't think anything is going on with the Skaines," Don Guido replied after a second spent considering. He hiccupped contemplatively.

"There's always something going on with the Skaines," Tabitha spat back grimly. "We just busted three Skaine ships doing a trade involving guns, drugs, and slaves."

"They're not from around here," Don Guido countered. "Just showed up. Might be a problem in the future."

"No, they won't. I killed them."

"Oh." He looked at her again with a new appreciation for how dangerous she was. "You're not going to kill *me*, are you?"

"No!" She stopped a moment and leaned forward. "Well, are you trading slaves or guns or anything?" she asked in a whisper.

"No." He shook his head. "I never wanted to get into that. I thought I would trade information, right? No guns. Just information. All safe." He shook his head again mournfully. "But people don't like facts. People always want to argue with you about facts. Some people want to kill you for facts. That's why Klio protects me."

"Mmm." Tabitha took a sip of her beer. "We won't argue with you about facts, anyway. Are you *sure* there's no Skaine Big Bad running around?"

He shook his head, then reconsidered. "Well, there's talk of someone called Rotciv. He sounds disgusting, but no one knows what kind of alien he is, and no one knows where he is. I'd tell you if I could. Would be worth a *lot* of money."

"Drink your water," Hirotoshi suggested.

Don Guido obediently started drinking.

Tabitha sat back in her seat smugly. "See? Rotciv—the next in the long line of Skaines I will kick back to their mother's womb."

"You don't know he's Skaine," Hirotoshi remarked reasonably.

"And there's Tiw's medicine," Don Guido added. "He had his whole supply stolen. They think it left on a ship called the *Geqward*. Here, wait a second." He tapped on the computer strapped to his arm, squinted to make out the keys, and tried again. "I sent the coordinates to your ship. You came on the *Achronyx*, right?"

Tabitha blinked. This guy was better than she'd thought. Hirotoshi gave her a meaningful look and picked his glass up—

Only to have it dashed out of his hands.

"You!" roared the alien who had attacked him a few days ago. "I told you I didn't like your face!"

"This should be good." Tabitha leaned out of the way as the alien grabbed Hirotoshi by the arm and hauled him into the space between the tables. She watched over her shoulder for a moment, then turned back to Don Guido. "Where were we?"

You should get out of there, Achronyx reported testily. *The inspector is not far away. He might see this fight.*

We'll deal with that if it happens.

Achronyx sighed.

Hirotoshi and the alien were still trading blows when a huge alien appeared in the doorway of the bar. He looked around with a keen eye, and Tabitha and Katsu noted him, then turned their faces the other way.

"I think that's the inspector," Tabitha muttered to Katsu. "Quick, out the back, while he's occupied with Hirotoshi."

"What about Hirotoshi?"

"He'll figure something out." They slipped around the back of the table, leaving cash for their drinks and whispering goodbye to Don Guido as they went.

Borven's gaze had immediately been drawn by the human fighting Okk, an alien he recognized. He stomped up to the two of them and pulled them apart.

"Here, now," he ground out. "What's going on here?" He looked around and chose a bystander at random. "You. What happened?"

Luckily, this bar wasn't one of the ones that hated inspectors. The patron coughed and shrugged his shoulders. "Well, sir, Okk went up to the alien there and said he didn't like the alien's face, then dragged him over there to fight. They hadn't been fighting long when you showed up."

Borven sighed. Okk was well-known on this station for starting fights with *anyone*.

Still, this was a human. He let Okk go and told him to sit down nearby, and leaned down to look at the human.

"You. You match the description of a human I am tracking." He looked around. "Are there more of you here?"

Hirotoshi looked around the bar, raising an eyebrow. "Apparently *not*," he allowed.

The inspector eyed him. He smelled a powerful liquor on his breath. "Hmm. Do you usually travel with two other humans?"

"No," Hirotoshi replied cautiously. "Sir," he added, echoing the etiquette of the other alien.

"Hmm." Borven folded his arms. "You match the description, though. Dark hair, pale skin."

"Ah." Hirotoshi smiled. "An understandable mistake. Many humans have this coloring. I'm afraid I really don't know anything else. This fight was…" He frowned at Okk. "I really don't know why it happened."

"Because he's Okk," Borven suggested resignedly. He waved to the door. "Very well, you can go."

"Thank you." Hirotoshi took his coat and left the bar, catching up with Tabitha and Katsu in the landing bay. "Kemosabe, you *abandoned* me."

"I knew you could take care of yourself, Number One." Tabitha led the way to the bridge. "Achronyx, lay in the coordinates from Don Guido and prepare to set out." She turned to Hirotoshi. "I already had backup plans if you got in trouble. We don't abandon *anyone*. However," she pointed to herself, "I'm much harder to hide. If he had seen me, we would have been screwed."

"Yes, Ranger Two." If Achronyx could do a snide voice,

he was doing it very well, and Tabitha rolled her eyes when he finished speaking. "Coordinates laid in."

A few minutes later, Achronyx announced, "Ranger Two, there is a holocall coming through for you." He sounded almost smug.

"Who is it?"

In answer, Achronyx brought up the video call. Borven Thod was glaring at the screen.

"Jackass," Tabitha muttered to Achronyx. To Borven, she smiled and waved. "Hi!"

Borven's eyes searched the frame and caught sight of Hirotoshi, then pointed. "There you are. I should have known not to trust you."

"Why shouldn't you have trusted me?" Hirotoshi asked. His voice was smooth and emotionless.

In response, Borven brought up a video that showed Tabitha, Hirotoshi, and Katsu walking into Yeven's Bar, and the events of the subsequent fight. It was sped up, and they watched it all the way through.

Tabitha leaned forward, watching as she traded hits and then kicked a couple of times. "Oh yes. That's the right angle. I'm going to have to move these pants up to being my regular leathers," she remarked to no one in particular. "Look at that! Damn, that ass is *hot!*" The screen cleared to show Borven's face, and Tabitha leaned back. "Ugh!" She waved a hand back and forth in front of the screen. "Not as pretty. Warn a girl next time, Inspector."

Borven glared back at the human female. "According to station law, I must ask you to come in for questioning."

"Nope," replied Tabitha cheerfully, waving her fingers. "Toodles. Places to go, bad guys to annoy."

"You will find that your ship is barred from leaving the station," Borven warned her.

"You'll find it's not," Tabitha countered. *It's not, right?*

I can get us out of here. Achronyx sighed. *If you want to be a criminal, that is.*

Tabitha chuckled. *That sounds great! Let's do that.*

I should have told you I couldn't.

I would have known you were lying and he will get over it. Tabitha grinned as the ship started to pull away from the station. Borven was furiously tapping at the keys of his console, and she snapped her fingers to get his attention.

His angry face popped onto the screen.

"Don't bother," she suggested. "We can get around any programming you put in place. We have to go now."

"I order you to re-dock," Borven shouted, furious.

"We'll be back soon." She terminated the call.

"Soon?" Hirotoshi echoed.

"Probably never. Well, hopefully never." Tabitha thought for a moment, then shrugged and pointed to the blank screen. "*He* doesn't need to know that. Anyway, come on, Achronyx, let's go find some stolen medicine. We might as well do something until we can track down Rotciv."

Rebus Quadrant, Themis Colony

The Tykis outpost had certainly seen better days.

That much was obvious from Nickie's impromptu tour of the site. The walls were grimy, half of the lights were flickering or dead, and it was apparent that there had been combat within the outpost's walls.

Despite all that, the colonists seemed cheerful when Nickie made it back to the main hall. Tired and a bit high on adrenaline, but cheerful. Nickie supposed winning their freedom back could do that, even if the job was only half done.

She strode through the room as if she owned it, grinning at the people who stopped to thank her. She found Grim at the center, surrounded by a flock of colonists. He was shaking hands and chatting, and getting a lot of slightly mystified looks.

"Never seen a Yollin before?" Nickie asked mildly as she came to a halt at the edge of the group.

"Very rarely," the woman to her left replied, still seeming breathless at everything that had happened. "Certainly not on our little colony."

Grim finally spotted Nickie and broke away from the colonists to approach her. "There you are," he commented wryly. "I was starting to think you'd launched yourself into space in a shuttle to get at the incoming Skaines early."

Nickie scoffed and punched his shoulder. "As if," she drawled and glanced around. "Where's, uh…Durq?" she wondered cautiously. "Is he getting up to some sort of trouble?"

Grim rolled his eyes. "He wanted to stay on the ship," he answered plainly. "Right about now, he's probably hiding under his bed. Or mine."

"Wait, you mean he does actually have his own room?" Nickie asked, bemused. "I thought you were kidding about that."

"The ship has twenty-four private quarters," Grim reminded her. "Including his."

Nickie grumbled something rather less than polite under her breath, but she let the topic go when Grim cleared his throat.

"Aaanyway," he continued, "there's someone you're going to want to meet. Follow me." He gestured for her to keep close with one hand and turned to make his way through the crowd.

"This is Keen," he offered when he slowed to a stop at the outskirts of a smaller group, where a handful of the colonists were muttering urgently amongst themselves until one of them—the Keen in question—pulled away from the group to speak with Nickie.

"Quite an impressive show you put on," he remarked.

Nickie shrugged broadly. "I do what I can. So, what's been going on here?"

Keen sighed slowly. "The initial invasion happened about two months ago. Everything we had mined and all of our nonessential equipment was confiscated, and we were put to work mining for them," he explained. "At least until recently, when our primary power generator died. The auxiliary shafts are basically dead, and the main shaft is only running on the barest amount of backup power. Working down there is effectively impossible. The only reason we've been able to hide down there without dying is that we know the layout so well."

He paused, glancing at Nickie to see if she had anything to contribute, but she simply motioned for him to carry on. He cleared his throat. "We weren't getting any work done for them anymore and they decided it would be too much of a hassle to get the mines up and running again, so they decided selling us off was the best way to handle things. We've gotten recent rumors of another Skaine ship coming to pick us up."

"Wait, what?" A young man, his clothes and his hair disheveled, practically tripped over, leading a young and equally disheveled woman by the hand. "Already?" he demanded.

"Raynard," Keen scolded mildly.

"Sorry, just—"

"What are we supposed to do now?" Adelaide asked fretfully.

Nickie cleared her throat to get their attention. "We'll just have to take out those fuckheads once they get here," she supplied, her tone almost pleasant. "Meredith can help with comm—"

"On it!" Raynard volunteered. "I've got all their signal data already. I was in charge of radio monitoring, and if I could do it with salvaged gear, I can definitely get the Skaines' communication gear working."

Nickie blinked at him before nodding. "Meredith, coordinate with him."

Raynard departed in a flash, leaving only Keen and Adelaide watching Nickie expectantly.

"He seems very helpful," Nickie commented after a moment.

"Where do you want us?" Keen asked. "We have a militia, though it's pretty informal."

Nickie shook her head slowly. "I work best on my own," she replied haltingly. Working on her own meant she didn't have to give complex commands.

"But what if they come into the mines?" Adelaide asked, wringing her hands. "You don't know your way around in there. You might need our help."

Nickie waved it off with a flick of her wrist. "My copilot can map it out for me in a jiffy," she replied. "Besides," she plucked one of her drones from her belt, "I have these."

Adelaide didn't seem convinced, glancing at the marble-sized ball in Nickie's hand. But she at least fell quiet, letting Keen ask, "Protocol for if we intercept any of the Skaines?"

"Kill them?" Nickie supplied. "I mean, I don't plan on taking any prisoners. We don't need any info from them, so we may as well just get rid of them."

She could practically see more questions building, and she decided it was time to nip it all in the bud.

"You just keep everyone tucked away," she commanded Keen, poking one finger into his chest. "I'm hardier than I look and I won't be needing much help, so just keep your people out of trouble and only come out if Meredith says I need help." She folded her arms over her chest and tried to sound stern. "Got it?"

"You're just one person," Adelaide fretted before Keen could say anything.

"I'm a little more than *that*," Nickie assured her, her gaze still locked on Keen.

"I understand." He sighed. "I'll keep everyone ready to move just in case."

Nickie clapped him on the shoulder. "Good man," she assured him, then began making her way back to the airfield.

As Nickie sauntered to the *Granddaughter* for some last-minute preparations, she couldn't quite help but point out, *You see? I was born to lead like this!*

Just try not to get yourself killed.

Meredith's request sounded more long-suffering than anything else.

Rebus Quadrant, Themis Colony, Lower Atmosphere

Boh'Locks 881 broke through the atmosphere with a bump and a rumble of metal as the engines adjusted, just as they had a thousand times before. After they descended a short way, Karvar glanced at his communications officer and commanded, "I expect us to have permission to land by the time we get to the airfield."

"Already on it, sir," the officer replied, adjusting his headset with one hand while the fingers of the other flew over the console.

The ship descended quickly, though well within the safety parameters. It wasn't long before Karvar could make out the outpost on the viewing screen. But despite the communications officer's assurances, there had been no update on whether the ship was clear to land.

Karvar looked slowly at the officer, his eyes narrowing slightly.

"Well?" he asked, drumming his fingers on his armrest. "What's the hold-up?"

With a quiet, "Um—" the officer glanced over his shoulder for a split second before turning to his console again with renewed efforts, as if the situation would resolve itself if he were simply emphatic enough. Of course, that wasn't actually the way it worked, and Karvar's impatience continued to mount until it was practically hovering over him like a dark and stormy cloud.

More than anything the communications officer seemed confused, tapping out commands in jerky movements. For the life of him, Karvar couldn't understand why. It had been a simple order, and it should have been a quick and simple response.

"Are we clear to land?" he asked sharply, getting up from his seat to look over the officer's shoulder. At a cursory glance, the signal exchange seemed uncharacteristically one-sided. "It's a routine check. What's the holdup?"

His communications officer shrugged and gestured to the console. "We're not getting a reply, sir. I've tried pinging the airfield four times, and there hasn't been an answer." He tapped out a few quick commands to send the inquiry again, and again there was no response.

"Make that five times." The officer sighed, but despite his apparent exasperation, he kept at it.

Karvar eyed the console warily before looking at the main viewing screen. He moved a few paces to the side, until he was standing behind the pilot's seat. "Take us down," he ordered, one hand on the back of the pilot's seat. "But be cautious. Something about this isn't right, and we don't know what kind of situation we're heading into."

The pilot nodded without taking his eyes off of the helm controls, offering a distracted, "As you command, sir." Karvar lingered behind the pilot's seat for a moment longer before returning to the captain's chair at the center of the bridge.

"Set scanners to their widest range," he commanded. "And keep an ear open for suspicious chatter."

Rebus Quadrant, Themis Colony

Incoming.

Meredith's warning was matter-of-fact and simple.

Raynard and I are picking up Skaine radio activity. The ship is preparing to land. They're already wary at the lack of a response.

Connect me to their comm, Nickie commanded, stretching her arms over her head before checking her equipment again to make sure she had everything. *I want them nervous, but not completely on guard. Nervous people are jumpy. Jumpy people make mistakes.*

You're connected.

Nickie pulled out her communicator as she made her

way to the airlock. She didn't like speaking the Skaine language—it was too guttural and harsh for even a syllable of it to sound attractive, so even their language sounded violent—but she knew it nonetheless. It came in handy from time to time.

"We're reading you," Nickie assured them. She swore she sounded like she was barking like a dog.

Can't you lower your voice any farther? You don't quite sound like a Skaine, and I can only modify your voice so much.

Irritated by the critique, Nickie tried.

"It took you long enough," the Skaine captain groused in reply. "What's the holdup?"

"There was a situation with the slaves. It's been dealt with. I'll meet you at the airfield." That said, she disconnected and opened the airlock's outer doors, just in time to see the Skaine ship landing.

Nickie began walking down the ramp.

Captain Karvar is attempting to contact you. He's trying to understand why a human is coming off a Skaine ship.

Then I guess I should go explain it to him in person, Nickie decided before she sprinted down the ramp and across the airfield.

The Skaines fired as soon as they saw her coming, and Nickie leapt and twisted through the air to dodge laser bolts. She ducked behind the ship that had brought the initial invasion and pulled her drones from her belt. As she huddled behind the ship, she tapped one of the drones on its top and cooed, "All right, you messy little fuckers. Do your thing."

She pitched the three metallic orbs into the air, and they zipped through the air toward the oncoming Skaines.

Nickie relegated the video feeds from the drones to the corner of her vision, letting Meredith monitor them for the time being. Each drone tore straight through the skull of a Skaine on the way down the gangplank, and three bodies dropped to the ramp. The doors began to close, but the drones zipped through at the last second.

She glanced at the feed every so often, watching the drones herd unfortunate Skaines still on the ship through the corridors until there were enough in one place to simply bounce around the room like a trio of pinballs. They ripped elegantly through skulls and torsos as they ricocheted. The ship would be empty in no time, so all Nickie had to focus on was the group making its way across the airfield.

Nickie peered carefully out of her hiding place, gun in hand. She ducked under a shot that passed a few inches past her scalp, and as she straightened back up, she fired at the barrels of fuel stored just a few yards from where Karvar's ship had landed.

A barrel exploded stupendously, leading to all the others exploding in rapid succession. The blasts launched debris and flaming gobs of fuel into the air to pelt the airfield with fire. The Skaines scattered, but four of them still wound up falling when they couldn't quite avoid the flaming liquid raining down on them. Soon the fire had halfway surrounded Karvar's ship, creeping along both sides of the gangplank.

Just five more of the ground team.

Nickie looked at the ship she was hiding behind and then climbed up the landing gear to drag herself into its undercarriage. She pressed her back flat to the jagged metal, arms and legs spread out to brace herself. She could hear the Skaines arguing amongst themselves beside the ship, trying to figure out who was going to drag her out of hiding. Finally, one of them stumbled forward after being pushed.

He made it two steps beneath the ship before Nickie hooked her knees around the ship's undercarriage and dropped to hang upside-down, just low enough to wrap her arms around the reluctant Skaine and haul him off the ground.

When the others opened fire he made a very nice shield, and when she dropped the body her gun was already in hand. Soon she was down to just three, and she dragged herself up into the undercarriage again.

She scuttled forward like an upside-down crab, ducking into the gap behind the landing gear and all but disappearing, so she was nowhere to be found when the three remaining Skaines finally trekked beneath the ship to find her.

She fired at one of them, shooting him through the top of the head before she backflipped down from the under-carriage. She landed on her feet, using another Skaine as a landing pad; his neck snapped loudly on impact.

Nickie blinked at the last Skaine, who had his gun on her from scarcely more than an arm's length away.

The world seemed to slow to a crawl as Nickie surged forward, flowing like water as she sidestepped the blast. She closed the space between them and snapped his elbow, slamming the flat of her hand against it and forcing it to bend in the wrong direction. His gun fell from his hand, and Nickie caught it, leveled it at his neck, and pulled the trigger. Scarcely more than a few seconds had passed before the Skaine crumpled to the ground in a heap and Nickie was alone again.

She was barely out of breath. Meredith interrupted her.

Captain Karvar is the only one remaining. He is still on the ship. I assume you would prefer I not handle him with your drones.

You got that right. That fucktard is mine, she confirmed, racing toward the gangplank. *But how do I get on? I can't open the doors from out here.*

The doors at the top of the gangplank sparked suddenly and slid partially open. She could hear the humming of her drones on the other side, and she could just barely smell smoking electronics over the smell of the fire.

With a wild grin, she sprinted up the gangplank and onto the Skaine ship, catching her drones out of the air as she passed them.

Nickie met the captain as he tried to flee to the bridge to barricade himself in. She caught him by the collar before he could get through the door, and with a vise-like grip on the back of his neck, she hauled him back toward the gangplank.

He fought the entire way and even managed to break her hold halfway there. He rounded on her, army knife in hand and outrage in his eyes. At such close range, it really wasn't a surprise that he managed to sink the knife into Nickie's hip. She yelped, the sound caught between pain and offense.

She lashed out, one hand yanking the knife out to let her healing kick in and the other curling into a fist to punch Karvar right in the face, although she pulled the punch so as not to kill him right then and there. It rattled him enough to keep him from struggling the rest of the way to the gangplank.

She had to pause for a moment once she got there, though. She hadn't expected the colonists to congregate on the airfield to watch the Skaine ship. A hush fell over them when the door opened and she appeared at the top of the gangplank with Karvar.

***

Grim watched from just below the Skaine ship's gangplank as Nickie frog-marched the captain halfway down it. Fire encroached on both sides of the gangplank, so the only ways to get away were back onto the ship—a dead end—or down the gangplank, right into the colonist's arms.

The captain, however, seemed disinclined to try to run. Either he was proud, or he simply knew it was no good by that point. Grim didn't know enough about Skaines to try to hazard a guess as to his thinking, and he was too busy straining to hear what they were saying to give the idea much attention.

"What do you think?" Nickie asked, and though her tone was friendly and pleasant enough, the grin on her face was like a barracuda's. "Anything you'd like to say for yourself?"

"Just get it over with," Karvar snapped. "You're the only one here who gives a shit about your posturing."

Nickie snorted out a laugh, though it wasn't a particularly cheerful sound. "Whatever you say," she agreed, and she sank his knife into his throat and yanked it to the side.

She sidestepped to avoid the spray of arterial blood, with limited success.

His body stayed upright for a moment, swaying slightly in place until Nickie placed two fingers in the middle of his chest and pushed. It tumbled over the side of the gangplank to burn up in the fire.

Grim cringed when the flames flashed higher for a few seconds, and as the colonists erupted into cheers, he looked away.

CHAPTER 17 TABITHA

Aboard the *Achronyx*

"I swear, every time we go to that place, I need three showers to get the stink off me," Tabitha complained, again to no one in particular. She appeared in the main conference room wearing new clothes. She looked around. "Are we close to the drop point?"

"Yes." Hirotoshi waved her over to look at the layout of a small town he was studying. He tapped a point on the screen. "Achronyx found a report of an abandoned colony at those coordinates and even a map of it. Our guess is that the thief, whoever he is, will set down at the south end of the colony and make the rendezvous before turning over the goods."

"Why wouldn't he bring the goods with him?" Tabitha frowned.

"The information Don Guido provided traces back to someone who usually operates alone. Achronyx can't find *any* criminal record for this guy."

A profile picture popped up, with the same pink-toned skin and delicate features as the alien who had attacked Tabitha in the bar.

"Those guys are dangerous!" she accused, staring at the picture on the screen. "How the hell do you tell them apart?"

Hirotoshi ignored her.

"Perhaps as a species they can be difficult, but there are no reported issues with this one," Katsu remarked, then shrugged. "His name is Hlith'ven. There's a weird click thing in the middle of it none of us can pronounce."

Tabitha scowled at the screen. "So he's good at hiding his tracks?"

"Maybe." Hirotoshi didn't look convinced. "I saw the security footage of him approaching the medical supply store, however, and he doesn't act like a hardened criminal."

"Hirotoshi is correct," Achronyx said over the speaker. "This alien is not very good at any of this. He rented the ship for more than necessary, meaning he did not have his own ship in the first place since we could find nothing about him outside of this effort. All of these actions are highly unusual for a criminal."

"Could be he's just never been caught." Tabitha chewed on the inside of her lips. "I think he's just sneakier than we might realize."

"Perhaps you are correct, Kemosabe." Hirotoshi dipped his head in her direction, then added, "But I doubt it."

She looked at him before asking, "Don't you have push-ups to do?" She jerked a thumb over her shoulder. "A thousand each for you and Katsu, and five hundred for Ryu?"

"In time. Perhaps after the battle, Kemosabe." Hirotoshi's lips moved in the direction of a tiny smirk. "We have arrived."

Tabitha stood up, scratching her face. "You're going to go for triple or nothing, aren't you?"

"I might have had that idea, yes." Hirotoshi headed for the armory.

Tabitha and the Tontos were geared up and ready to go without much time spent, and they headed out into the ruins of the colony to wait for their contact to arrive. When they looked around, the buildings seemed fairly well-preserved, some with windows boarded up and For Sale signs written in seven different languages in others.

One of them reminded Tabitha of Morse code.

"This place is weird." Tabitha slowly turned in place, looking at the complete lack of people. "How does a whole colony just stop being a thing?"

It was on a trade route, Achronyx answered a moment later. *After one of the treaties fell through between two major systems, it wasn't a convenient stopping point anymore. It gradually faded. There was no major catastrophe, which is why you see multiple stages of abandonment.*

Tabitha nodded.

She had seen similar things happen in Buenos Aires. Neighborhoods and small towns near the city would stop being a destination for some reason or another, and half the buildings would go derelict.

Of course, in her experience, other people moved in

and started their own black market economy. That was just more difficult in space.

"He's coming in," Ryu reported. There was a boom somewhere above, and Tabitha and the Tontos *moved*, hiding inside one of the abandoned buildings while they waited.

It wasn't long before their target appeared. He had dressed in nondescript gray clothes, the usual station-worker's uniform, but they only served to emphasize his pink skin.

He looked very delicate and nervous. His eyes moved erratically, and he stumbled twice as he walked down the street.

"Hey, you!" Tabitha stepped into the street, and he looked at her in confusion. "I hear you stole medicine from Tiw." She put a hand on her waist. "Want to explain that?"

Clearly, the alien did *not* want to stand around and talk with her. He panicked and took off.

"Oh, for fuck's sake!" Tabitha sprinted after him. "Come on! I don't want to get dirty." She tackled him to the ground. To her relief he didn't pull out any of the glass knives, but instead cowered in front of her, arms wrapped around his head.

"Please," he whimpered.

Tabitha leaned close to him, knocking the dust off of her pants, "Please *what*?" she asked as the guys caught up with them.

"I've never done anything like this before!" he answered, still holding his arms around his head.

"I told you," Hirotoshi said, faintly smug.

Tabitha, sensing defeat, pointed down at him. "He could

be lying!" she said, although her eyes gave away what she really thought.

"I'm not lying!" Hlith'ven turned and sat up. He looked at Tabitha and Hirotoshi. "He's right. He's..." His eyes narrowed. "You're male, yes?"

"Yes," Hirotoshi agreed patiently while Tabitha and Ryu snickered. He just looked at them and both stopped, deciding that staring at the alien was a better choice at the moment.

Tabitha tried again, waving her hand in front of her. "*Nothing* he can say is going to convince me to let him go."

"I was just doing this to pay off my debt to Rotciv," Hlith'ven explained.

"Then again," Tabitha blew out a breath of annoyance, "I've been known to be wrong."

"Yes, but you've never been known to *admit* it," Katsu supplied.

She glared at him and then looked back at Hlith'ven. "What's this about Rotciv? You know who that Skaine son of a bitch is?"

"I don't know if he's Skaine," Hlith'ven replied.

"He is," Tabitha told him, her previous mistake forgotten already as she answered confidently.

The alien stared at her. "O-okay. Anyway, my parents' colony was getting attacked by slavers all the time, so we hired some people to guard it. They charged way more than they said they were going to after they fought off an attack, and the next thing I know, I'm being contacted by this Rotciv guy."

Katsu turned to the side and whispered to Ryu, "How does this thing translate 'okay?'"

Ryu shrugged. The technology worked—at least for the most part—and that was all he needed.

Tabitha crouched and glared at Hlith'ven. She rolled her eyes when he gave a yip of terror.

"Okay, I'm beginning to believe you," she looked up at Hirotoshi. "He really doesn't seem like he—"

"He sold us out!" Tabitha's better hearing caught an alien talking behind them. "Look, it's those *humans!* Get them and get the merchandise!"

The first shots cracked into the air and Tabitha snatched Hlith'ven by the collar to drag him into a nearby house. She pointed at him and then the floor. "Stay the fuck here! I can't let you die until we find out more about Rotciv, so keep your damned head down!"

Hirotoshi and Ryu had taken shelter on the other side of the street, and Ryu looked out, aimed his Jean Dukes, and fired. The alien who had been yelling orders, bare skin speckled and otherwise covered in bristly fur, screamed and fell.

"That is for attacking us without provocation!" Ryu called to the rest. "I suggest the rest of you go back to your ship and leave. The deal is off."

"Fuck you, motherfucker!" the call came back.

"And that?" Katsu asked. "How many aliens can have fornicating with one's mother as a thing?"

"*Rude.*" Tabitha popped out of the doorway of her shelter to shoot the one who had yelled and ducked back in as several of them fired at her. The slams of the projectiles splattering stone chips were annoying enough without the actual damage from being hit by one.

They had brought shields with them, some sort of

collapsible contraption that sprang up to give them cover in the open street. She doubted it would do much against Jean Dukes over time, but it was a nifty thing.

"Hirotoshi!"

"Yes, Kemosabe?"

"We should bring some of our shields next time."

It was a damned shame. It wasn't like they didn't *have* the shields. They just didn't usually use them except during ship actions.

Tabitha checked her pockets. Nope, she didn't have any.

"Yes, Kemosabe." Hirotoshi shot two more, and Ryu picked off a third.

The traders had come around their barriers and were sprinting up the street toward Hlith'ven's ship. They must have decided that their random shots had taken out some of their adversaries, or perhaps they thought they could shoot them when they came out into the street.

Either way, they were wrong.

Hirotoshi and Ryu stepped out into the street, swords flashing in the sunset.

Three had come past the barriers to get to the ship. Ryu took two steps and vaulted into the air so that he and Hirotoshi could attack from opposite sides. They did not want to drive any of their enemies into the building with Hlith'ven.

The merchant closest to Ryu managed to draw his gun, but Ryu slashed at his arm. Blood splattered when the hand still holding the butt of the pistol dropped into the dirt. The merchant screamed in pain as Ryu cut him down with a return slice.

Hirotoshi took out one merchant almost instantly, but the second had a grenade launcher pointed right at him.

"Don't move!" the merchant ordered. "You just stay right where you are. We're going to take that merchandise—"

He didn't get a chance to finish his orders. Ryu stabbed him through the back, yanked down to pull the aim up on the launcher and pulled his sword out with a slight twist to break the vacuum as the merchant fell.

Ryu nodded at Hirotoshi, and both of them ran for the shields.

Tabitha had left Hlith'ven where he was and climbed up to the roof of her building. Now she ran across it and leapt down to the street behind the shields.

"Nice to see you," she told Hirotoshi and Ryu. "Wondered when you'd show up."

The five remaining merchants screamed. Two of them dropped their weapons, put their hands up, and cowered.

The other three made the very unwise decision to try to take Tabitha and the Tontos down. One of them grabbed two guns and tried to fire them both at the same time.

"Seriously?" Tabitha asked, looking at the merchant's grip on his pistols. He wasn't used to holding guns, and Hirotoshi merely ducked under the pistol's aim as he fired.

Not only was the merchant horrible at aiming, but the recoil from the two pistols also sent both shots wide and the alien went ass over teakettle. One of the shots hit the building where Hlith'ven was hiding and they heard him scream, but given where it hit the building, the scream was almost certainly just surprise on Hlith'ven's part.

"Idiot," Ryu muttered.

"That is our ally you are speaking about," Hirotoshi replied.

"Ryu is right." Tabitha ripped the arm off one of the fighters and beat him over the head with it before taking his gun away. She checked the settings, aimed, and shot him with it. "*These* bastards are stupid. *Hlith'ven* is an idiot."

Ryu slashed through the neck of the last fighting merchant. He fell to the ground with a gurgle, his blood splattering near Tabitha, who jumped out of the way.

She pointed her Jean Dukes at the two remaining merchants. "Unlike your friend, I actually *can* handle two guns at once. So," she waved her pistols, "talk. Why should we let you live?"

"We didn't shoot at you." one of them argued. He was a small alien with bluish skin and multifaceted eyes. "I swear! We had guns, but we didn't fire. We've never done anything like this before."

The other alien nodded nervously. He looked to be the same species as Don Guido, scrawny and green.

"Have we met you before?" he asked Tabitha. "The rest of them seemed to know who you are. But he's right, we're both new."

Tabitha reached out in disgust and slapped both aliens. "Go home," she ordered, waving a hand. "Go back to your ship and go home. You're not cut out for this life."

They went, looking dazed, and Tabitha holstered her Jean Dukes and walked back to the building Hlith'ven was hiding in and stepped inside. A moment later, she hauled him into the street once more.

She barely let him catch up. "Come on, Hlith'ven, let's go get that medicine unloaded."

"But...but why?" Hlith'ven hurried along beside her, trying to keep her grip on his collar from making him trip. "You sent the merchants away." He gave a little moan And put hands up to his face. "How am I going to pay Rotciv off now?"

"We're taking the medicine," Tabitha explained to him, "and giving it back to Tiw. Don't think of stealing it again, or it will go *very* poorly for you."

Hlith'ven began to protest, pointing behind him. "But what if—"

Tabitha shook her head, her hair swishing. "I don't want to hear it. We'll figure out something." She stepped up to a new level in the ground and yanked Hlith'ven along with her.

"But if I don't do this, I'll have to do the weapons thing he wanted me to do!"

Tabitha stopped, causing Hlith'ven to run ahead of her, choke on his collar, and fall on the ground. She considered his words as he picked himself up, then put her hands on her waist and leaned in. "Did he tell you where the deal was going down?"

Hlith'ven checked his scraped skin. "Yes. I thought if I showed up with the money he wanted, he wouldn't make me do the gunrunning."

"Listen to me carefully," Tabitha told him. "You. Are. Stupid."

The guys had been walking behind them as Tabitha had been dragging Hlith'ven to his ship.

Hirotoshi sighed.

"He is!" Tabitha protested, pointing to the alien. "You know he is."

"Why am I stupid?" Hlith'ven asked.

She turned back to him, but Ryu was the one who spoke.

"Because someone like Rotciv doesn't just get you to do *one* thing," Ryu explained. "He's going to make you do other stuff as well. In fact, showing him you had other ways to get the money might have been the worst thing you could have done."

Tabitha and Hirotoshi nodded.

"How about this?" Tabitha asked. "We'll pay off your debt for you."

Hlith'ven looked at her, and then at the others. "What? Why?"

"Well..." She wiggled her fingers in a fashion Hlith'ven didn't recognize. "Rotciv isn't going to be bothering you anymore."

Hlith'ven entirely failed to grasp the nuance and gaped. "Why would you do that for me?"

"Because," she waved to the others and herself, "we're very nice people." She slung an arm around his shoulders. "Now, why don't you tell me where this deal is going down? Is Rotciv going to be there?"

"Yes. He said he wanted to meet me." Hlith'ven's shoulders drooped.

"Yeah, I bet."

Hlith'ven lived on a well-traveled station and was clearly terrified by Rotciv. He could do a lot for the crime lord. He just hadn't counted on Hlith'ven running into someone like Tabitha.

"It's in the Q'abis system," Hlith'ven, his voice soft, explained. "I was supposed to pick up the weapons from them and run them over to another place. They said they'd tell me when I showed up." He fished in a pocket and took out a simple tablet, powering it up. "Look, here are the coordinates for the rendezvous. I was going to go as soon as I got the money."

"Good, good." Tabitha copied the coordinates from Hlith'ven's tablet and continued walking him back to his ship, from which Jun and Katsu had unloaded all the medicine.

They gave her a thumbs-up, and she turned back to Hlith'ven. "Ok, we have a problem. One is *you* know too much, but I need you to go back to what you were doing. So, I'm going to give you an out, so to speak.

He watched her, not sure what to think at the moment.

"Here is the story, and you need to work it," she told him. "You brought us here on a sightseeing tour," Tabitha explained, as Hirotoshi and Ryu stepped up behind Tabitha. "We're thinking of buying this colony, you see."

"Oh?"

"Tabitha." Hirotoshi sighed, "There is no way he is going to be able to remember this."

Tabitha's lips pressed together. "Ok, new story. You stole shit, and we used you to find them." She pointed to the bodies in the street. "You need to lie low for helping an undercover sting operation." She sent contact information to his tablet. "Those who need to know can contact us here. We will get the medicine to the right place and take care of Rotciv."

He looked at her dubiously for a moment., then leaned to the side, looking at the dead bodies. "Would you let me know when you have him?"

Tabitha smiled, "That's the right attitude, and you bet." She waved him toward his ship. "Now shoo."

The team watched as Hlith'ven flew away. "He is clearly not an accomplished pilot," Ryu commented when the ship turned a hundred and eighty degrees and headed in the opposite direction.

"Clearly," Tabitha agreed. She clapped her hands as she turned toward the *Achronyx*. "Well, let's go get this Skaine bastard," she suggested, grinning at Hirotoshi. "And then return the medicine, of course. A good deed done, and another Skaine crossed off the list. It will be a good day."

Hirotoshi snorted. "Would you like to go triple or nothing on whether or not Rotciv is Skaine?"

Her feet crunched on the gravel. "Hell *yeah*, I'll take that bet." She waved toward the ship. "Katsu still has to do push-ups, though. And Ryu."

"I will also come up with a bet," Ryu countered. "Perhaps we could bet on...the types of guns they're smuggling?"

Tabitha shook her head. "Nope. Push-ups for you."

"Well, what about—"

"Get started, Ryu." Tabitha walked up the gangway. "I'm not going to have Achronyx land until you've finished."

CHAPTER 18 NICKIE

Rebus Quadrant, Themis Colony

Nickie heaved a sigh and slumped into an empty chair. It hadn't been empty a moment ago, but she was willing to assume that whoever had been sitting in it wouldn't mind giving it up. It was for a good cause. It would have been almost relaxing, if not for the bustle and noise of the colonists cheering and crying and endlessly talking. Their voices seemed to bounce off the walls of the main hall.

We did good work today, she mused eventually, *but this colony is still going to be in the Skaines' database.*

Not if I have anything to do with it.

There were very few systems that Meredith couldn't have her way with. The colony would probably be off the database and virtually erased from Skaine memory within the next ten minutes.

Though I suspect you're going to need to have a chat with the colonists if you don't want anything like this happening again.

Meredith was just offering practical advice, but Nickie

heaved a sigh all the same, nodding in silent agreement. She gave herself a few more minutes to just sit and take a load off before she levered herself back to her feet and went to find Keen. If she sat too long she would probably fall asleep where she was sitting, and no one needed her wasting that sort of time.

He was easy enough to find. He was at the center of the largest crowd of colonists as they all vied for his attention. Nickie supposed he had a lot of work ahead of him to get the colony back on track, but he could handle the minutiae later. She tapped him on the shoulder and crooked her finger in a "follow me" gesture, turning on her heel and leading him to a slightly quieter hallway.

"Quite a performance you put on out there," he remarked once they came to a halt, sounding as if he were caught between wariness and admiration. Not an unreasonable response to a public execution, Nickie supposed, though she would have preferred the admiration.

She shrugged and waved it off with a prideful sort of flippancy. "What can I say? I'm happiest when the spotlight is on me." Her eyebrows rose as she asked, "But what about you? If nothing else, this has taught me that the spotlight is your worst fucking enemy."

Keen laughed ruefully and dragged a hand through his hair. "That would seem to be the case," he agreed. "I suppose we'll get the generator fixed and find out where all our equipment's been stashed; see if we can't get things back up and running in peace. We'll need to get some attention back on us after that if we want to start trading with the ore distributors again. This colony doesn't run on goodwill, after all. We need to start bringing money in again as soon as we can."

He recoiled slightly when Nickie held a finger up in his face.

"Actually," she corrected him sharply, "your *first* course of action is going to be getting some goddamn colonial defense weaponry." She dropped her hand, instead folding her arms over her chest as she tried her hardest to look stern.

"Meredith and I can get you off the Skaine database without a problem," she continued, not yet mentioning that Meredith had probably already removed them from the database. "But if you go right back to mining and trading like nothing ever happened, you're just going to attract someone else's attention and this entire mess is going to start all over again." She paused for a moment to let that sink in. "You need to get your hands on some AA weapons to, uh...*discourage* anyone else who might decide you're an easy target."

Keen was quiet for a moment as he turned the idea over. "Okay, so what do you have in mind?" He held an arm out, gesturing toward the main hall. "The outpost is a mess right now. We can't just pull anti-aircraft artillery out of a mine shaft. We're going to *have* to start operations up again just to afford these defenses."

Nickie hummed a thoughtful note and tapped her chin with one finger. "I have an idea about that," she replied after a moment. "Just let me talk things over with Meredith."

She turned away, but before she could say anything, Meredith beat her to it.

You found something relevant in the database?

Maybe. Nickie was no good at playing innocent, and she gave it only a half-hearted attempt. In the corner of her vision, she could see the database scrolling rapidly before it stopped on the entry that had caught her attention. There was a beat before Meredith dared to comment.

Please tell me you aren't planning on intercepting a weaponry exchange with the Leath. Please tell me you aren't that crazy.

Of course, I'm not crazy, Nickie assured her. *I mean, you live in there. You know how stable my mind is.*

Notably, she did *not* say that she wasn't planning on tangling with the Leath in the near future.

That's exactly what worries me.

I'm very fucking offended. The reply was delivered as close to deadpan as Nickie could manage when she wasn't speaking out loud.

Don't blame me when you get eaten as a side dish. You have been pressing your luck, and it will be entirely your fault.

That's what you're here for, Nickie reminded her, trying to sound as sweet as she could. *You'll help. You wouldn't leave me in the lurch with the Leath, would you?* Had it been a physical conversation, she would have been batting her eyelashes.

Meredith was silent for a very long moment after that.

I suppose I would be in just as much trouble if you got into trouble. I don't have much of a choice here since I know you aren't going to change your mind.

You're my favorite, Nickie assured her earnestly. *Glad that's settled.*

She shook her head briefly and turned toward Keen

again, who looked quietly baffled at Nickie's strange behavior.

"Okay!" Nickie declared, planting her hands on her hips. "You just stay focused on getting the colony back up and running and keeping all of your people in order. All right? I'll handle the weapons. I'll be back once I have them."

Keen seemed even more confused. "You can just...do that?" he asked, bewildered. "How? Honestly, who *are* you?"

Nickie grinned and folded her arms. "You can call me Ranger Two," she answered. "You may have heard of me?"

Keen blinked at her uncomprehendingly, and Nickie's face fell.

"Really?" she asked, trying very hard not to whine and not succeeding. "Not even a glimmer of recognition?" She swore to herself she wouldn't pout in front of the leader of the colony. She could sulk about it later, back on the ship with Grim. He would be able to appreciate her disappointment.

Keen shrugged. "You might have noticed we're a little isolated," he pointed out. "That didn't happen by accident."

Nickie huffed out an aggravated sigh and grumbled under her breath, "So much for that introduction," before she straightened back up and dragged a hand down her face. "Whatever! Not important! The important part is that I'll handle getting you those defensive measures and you can keep everything here calm in the meantime."

Keen nodded in easy agreement. "I'm certainly not going to complain," he replied wryly. "I take it that means you'll be on your way, then?"

"Once I find where Grim wandered off to, yeah," Nickie

confirmed, already starting to head back to the main hall. "Wasting time isn't really my favorite hobby."

"Fair enough." He sighed good-naturedly. "Just look for the largest crowd of gawkers, and you'll likely find him at the center of it."

Nickie flashed him a cheerful thumbs-up and loped back into the main hall to track her Yollin companion down.

As suspected, he was surrounded by a gaggle of colonists, still gawking at the novelty of seeing a Yollin in person. Extricating him from the group very nearly took as much skill as the entire confrontation with the Skaines. By the time she managed to rescue him, they both offered regretful goodbyes. She was almost convinced she would need to smuggle him off the planet.

In contrast, she felt a little underappreciated, considering it was she who had gone through all the trouble to save all their asses.

As soon as they were out of the main hall, they made a beeline back to the *Penitent Granddaughter* as if both of their asses were on fire and they were trying to outrun the blaze.

Rebus Quadrant, Themis Colony, Aboard the *Penitent Granddaughter*

The doors to the bridge slid open, and Nickie and Grim stepped through.

Lefty and Brandy followed them and vacuumed up the dirt, ash, and blood they tracked in. With a stretch, Nickie tumbled down into the captain's chair and turned her attention to the main viewing screen. Meredith was already powering it on, and a moment later the airfield was on the display. Most of the colonists had gathered there to wave the ship off.

"You think I should tell them?" Nickie mused, leaning an elbow on one of the armrests and propping her chin in her hand. She smiled impishly.

"You may as well," Meredith replied. "Who knows how long it will take them to figure it out on their own if you don't?"

"I feel like I'm missing something." Grim sighed, slumping down at what was supposed to be the first officer's station.

"You'll figure it out in a second," Nickie assured him. "Mere, patch me through to Keen's communicator and put him on speaker."

"Of course," Meredith agreed. Just a few seconds later Keen's voice came through the bridge speakers.

"I kind of figured you had said everything you needed to say," he remarked, sounding vaguely amused. "Just can't bear to say goodbye to our little spit of rock, then?"

Nickie snorted. "Not quite," she drawled in return. "I just wanted to say that you should probably go check on the main generator down in the mine. You never know when something might change."

"I'll get someone right on that," he replied slowly, suspicion creeping into his words. Nickie grinned and kept an eye on the viewing screen, spotting where Keen was when one of the colonists abruptly went haring away from the crowd and toward the mines.

"It must be quite a big deal if you're calling just to tell me about it," Keen remarked.

She hummed a low note, but simply remarked, "Who am I to say?" with a lofty sort of innocence. "What's important varies from person to person, doesn't it?"

Keen sighed slowly. "You're not just going to tell me," he stated, though it was perhaps supposed to be a question.

"Nope," Nickie answered cheerfully. "You'll know soon enough."

Keen grumbled, good-natured but still sullen nonetheless, and hung up. Nickie leaned toward the viewing screen in anticipation, her grin getting brighter as she saw the person who had been sent to check the generator pelting back toward the airfield at top speed.

There was a moment of calm as the messenger filled Keen in on the situation, and then a cheer broke out, loud enough that it was audible from the bridge of the ship. Nickie couldn't quite hold in a burst of laughter, and a moment later Keen called her.

"You sly dog!" he crowed, laughter in his words. "How did you manage to get your hands on one of those?"

"Oh, well, you know." Nickie sighed, playing coy for all of three seconds before her grin stretched even wider. "It's not like any of the Skaines need that ship anymore, which means the ship doesn't need any of the generator cells in its core. I just liberated one of them for a better cause."

Keen laughed incredulously. "We're going to owe you even more when you get back with the weapons," he mused, though he didn't sound bothered about it.

"Consider it a gift," Nickie assured him primly. "That means you're obligated to enjoy it."

Keen snorted, and his voice was distant as he leaned away from his communicator to shout to the crowd, "No work until tomorrow, you hear me? Each and everyone one of you is under orders to relax!"

As the crowd cheered, Nickie quietly disconnected. The ship took off shortly after that, and she watched the crowd wave them on their way until they were all too small to see.

Rebus Quadrant, Aboard the *Penitent Granddaughter*

"You never do anything small, do you?" Grim observed, his words fond.

Nickie scoffed. "Life is too short as it is. I'm not going to make it seem even shorter by being small about anything," she insisted, tipping her head back enough that she could get a look at him. "Speaking of small things, will—what's his name?—Durq be joining us sometime today?"

Grim hummed a negative. "Probably not. For a Skaine, he's pretty goddamn timid. Honestly, for *any* species he's kind of timid." He shrugged. "Food for thought, I suppose."

Nickie didn't say anything, but she did at least grunt in acknowledgment. Grim took it as a prompt to continue.

"About whether all of them are slavers and mercenaries and weapons dealers, I mean," he added, his tone slightly pointed.

Nickie shrugged one shoulder and mumbled a noncommittal, "I guess."

Grim wasn't an idiot. He could recognize that he wasn't going to get any other reply out of her, so he filed that detail away for later and let the topic drop. At the same time Nickie yawned so widely that her jaw cracked, and she slumped down in her seat.

Grim could see where it was going. She wasn't going to

be a conversationalist for much longer. Wisely he decided it would be better to just throw in the towel early.

"I could go get some dinner ready," he suggested, heading toward the door before he finished making the suggestion. "After feeding the rioting masses without much of an issue, just feeding a couple people will be a snap. Plus, I found a few steaks in the freezer when I was cleaning up," he explained, pausing at the door and turning to look back at her. "I could do something with those and a nice Beaujolais?"

Nickie hummed in absentminded agreement, flapping one hand at him in a manner that wasn't quite dismissive but came very close. "Yeah, sounds great," she replied. It was unclear as to whether she had registered a word Grim had said to her. She yawned again. "While you're doing that, you mind if I…" Her voice trailed off, and she tipped her head back to look at him with as little effort as she could get away with.

"You go ahead and put your feet up." Grim sighed. "I'll wake you up when there's food. Sound like a plan?"

She offered him a brief thumbs-up and kicked her feet up, crossing her ankles on top of Brandy's rounded head. Grim turned away from her to open the door, and by the time he stepped out into the corridor, she was snoring.

He chuckled quietly and took his time getting to the galley and getting everything ready.

CHAPTER 19 TABITHA

Hlith'ven was late. Rotciv paced up and down, growled slightly to himself, and checked his timepiece.

Hlith'ven would be a good contact. He'd known that at once. The alien clearly thought he was too small to be important. Rotciv smirked.

He rather liked those who didn't know their importance. It made keeping them under his thumb that much easier.

For years, he'd had designs on Farha Station. It was nicely situated, just at the edge of a major shipping lane. Enough trade already came through there to make the station administrators rich, and any number of accidents could befall ships that would then seek refuge there.

If Rotciv controlled the station, he'd get his hands on a lot of cash and goods, plus he'd have access to the information flowing through this sector.

He'd heard there were good information brokers at Farha Station.

Hlith'ven might be able to give him the station. He was right—as an Ulie, no one took him very seriously, except for that damned militant religious sect. Ulies were delicate and unsuited to fighting for the most part, and Rotciv had always thought weakness in fighting ability made a person weak in *every* way.

After all, how could you trust someone who wouldn't swing a punch to defend themselves? Who would bow and scrape and say anything to avoid a fight?

Those were the people who liked to keep secrets and spin schemes.

Of course, those were also the people who kept Rotciv in business, so he couldn't really complain. Shove a gun in someone's face and threaten to pull the trigger, and they often fell all over themselves to give you whatever you wanted.

He shrugged. Not his problem. The universe supported those who supported themselves. Those with the bigger guns or bigger threats won.

He was sure that in Hlith'ven he'd picked his target well, but now the Ulie was late.

Rotciv frowned. "Did you grow a spine, you little bug?"

The alien's fingers twitched near his sidearm. "Or have you turned me in?" If he had, Hlith'ven was going to be very, very sorry. For that matter, his whole *family* was going to be sorry.

Rotciv never missed an opportunity to make a point.

"There's a ship coming in," one of his soldiers called.

Finally! Rotciv grunted and went to stand at the lookout point, his arms crossed. When he saw the ship, though, his scowl turned into a look of disbelief.

This was Hlith'ven's ship? It was a sleek thing, engines glowing in a way Rotciv had never seen. His face contorted in confusion. *What kind of fuel did it use? And what were those weapons there?* It had a red band across the nose that he didn't like much.

Rotciv turned and spat to the side. *I can paint over that.*

He stomped down to the landing area as the gangway opened, then stopped and gestured to his soldiers not to load up the guns just yet.

The one coming out wasn't Hlith'ven.

It was a human. Well, *five* humans, to be exact. The one in the lead was shorter than the others and much curvier under the black clothing. Rotciv guessed that one was female. His eyes narrowed. *The others would be males, then.*

But none of them were Hlith'ven, and none looked as if they would be easily intimidated.

Meanwhile, the human woman was looking around in increasing disgust. She pointed at Rotciv.

"You. Where's Rotciv?" she asked.

He pushed his voice lower; low enough to grate on his throat. *"I'm* Rotciv."

"No fuckin' way." She started to laugh. She looked at one of the men, back at Rotciv, and then back to her man again. "He's not Skaine. I can't fucking *believe* it. I'll find something else to bet on, though. Quadruple or nothing?"

"No deal," her companion responded, smiling. "Would you like to start now, Kemosabe? Three thousand."

She looked affronted. "Three thousand, you ass? It's fifteen hundred." She shook her head. "I didn't just fall off the truck and bump my head."

Her companion shook his head. "That's triple the *orig-*

inal bet. Triple from the second bet would be *three* thousand."

The other males started laughing as she said something Rotciv couldn't decipher.

Probably cursing. His implant wasn't good at rare words like epithets. Although why someone would want to have relations with their...

He shook his head as he struggled to follow their conversation. He pulled his gun out of its holster and cocked it to get their attention.

All of their heads turned, their eyes narrowed and their hands dropped to their guns. Two had them out and aimed at him before he could blink.

Rotciv smiled, uncocked his gun, and let it slide back into the holster before he took his hand off his weapon deliberately.

"Now is not the time for arguing," he suggested. "Why are *you* here?"

"Oh, right." The woman crossed her arms. "We're here to make sure you and Hlith'ven don't have any debt between you. We also thought we'd take those weapons."

The soldiers obligingly picked up the crates, and Rotciv jabbed his hands at them.

"No deal," he argued. "Hlith'ven's debt won't be paid off by just this job. I was thinking of *employing* him for a long, long time. He needs to run this job himself...and then come back to get the next instructions."

"I think you've misunderstood." The woman cocked her head to the side. "I said we were here to make sure you and Hlith'ven didn't have any debt, and to take the weapons.

You seem to think I meant that I'd be working for you in Hlith'ven's place."

Rotciv frowned. "*Isn't* that what you meant?"

"Not exactly, no." She smiled, and her hand went to her weapon. "You see, I guessed that you'd want Hlith'ven to keep working for you after this. The way I see it, the only way his debt to you is cleared…is if *you die.*"

"Big mistake." Rotciv gestured behind his back for his soldiers to arm themselves. She and her men hadn't gone on the attack yet, and he thought he still had time to show them that they were outnumbered.

Now, if he could just lure them away from the ship, so he could take it…

"Why's it a mistake?" the human asked, her eyes widening. She crossed her arms and leaned back slightly, deliberately insulting.

Rotciv turned around, pointing to his people. "You see the numbers here?" He gestured as he turned back. "I'm pretty sure you can, right?"

She shrugged. "I see the numbers, but do you see the *odds?*"

"What does *that* mean?"

The human raised an eyebrow. "Asswipe. I'm Ranger Two of the Etheric Empire, and *you* are going to come in and answer for your crimes." She leaned forward and gave him a feral smile. "I'm doing this one by the book. For *Shin.*"

He had no idea what that last part meant, but he had no plans to let her take him in anywhere.

"Attack!" he yelled as he jumped for cover.

Tabitha and the Tontos sprinted for cover on the other side of the landing area, dodging as shots rang out.

"Remember not to kill him," Tabitha yelled, then banged her head on a rock as she scrambled. "Much!" she amended, rubbing her head. "*Fuck, that hurts!*"

"Remember that we're hiding behind a crate of what might be ammunition," Hirotoshi pointed out.

"Well, shit! Let's look." Tabitha hauled one of the sides of the crate down and swore as weapons tumbled out. "Dammit, that was my kneecap! Motherfucker. Okay, some ammunition, and… Hey, a rocket launcher!"

"Kemosabe." Hirotoshi lunged out to fire several shots, then ducked back behind the crate once again. "They're advancing, and I would like to point out that our cover is now an *empty* crate."

Tabitha looked at the crate and flinched when a hole was blown in it, throwing splinters toward her. "Right." She waved a hand. "Let's all go behind that concrete barrier when I give the signal." Tabitha pointed toward a concrete barrier several steps to their right.

She swung the rocket launcher onto her shoulder and lifted herself up from behind cover. "What's up, jackoffs?" she asked, flicking the cover off the arming switch.

It's the purple button. Achronyx told her.

Tabitha looked down. She had been going for the red button. *I knew that.*

She touched the purple button and there was a WHOOMPH as a rocket headed toward those running, who were having issues with the dense jungle.

Dropping her spent rocket launcher, she grabbed weapons on her way to the new cover.

"Okay, new plan." Tabitha dropped an armful of guns on the ground. "We play with all the fun toys!"

Hirotoshi sighed, but the others were already sorting through the pile of guns.

"Oooh, I like this one," Tabitha announced. She sighted something through the scope, loaded some ammunition into it, and took a shot at one of the trees behind them to test the accuracy.

"Oh, shit," she murmured.

A portion of the tree's trunk exploded into wood chips, and Tabitha hastily pulled Hirotoshi, who was busy looking toward the enemy, out of the way of the falling trunk.

"My bad," she told him as he looked at the tree and then back at her.

He blinked twice. "Kemosabe, you have Jean Dukes."

Tabitha shrugged. "They're not as much fun for midrange stuff. I didn't know we were going to be having a rifle battle! Next time I'll come prepared, don't worry. Let's go get the asshole, but try not to shoot him."

"That shouldn't be hard," Katsu quipped. "He's too much of a coward to shoot at us."

Tabitha lifted her head up long enough to see over the concrete. "Figures, huh? Jackass."

She took the new gun and crept to the side of the concrete barrier. Taking careful aim at the forest behind the people who were shooting at them, she fired.

With a creak and a *BOOM*, one of the big branches of a huge tree twisted and fell, slamming against the trunk and then tipping onto the line of soldiers. They scattered, yelling, and Tabitha chuckled.

"Wasn't that great?" She looked at Hirotoshi. "Got the idea when that tree nearly fell on you." He eyed her. "What? You always say never to waste any knowledge. I'm just following your dictates."

He gave her a look.

Tabitha flinched when a couple of rounds impacted near her cover. "Damn, too serious, Big H. I think you should lighten up a bit. Have some laughs!"

Hirotoshi turned to his side. "Why does she find gun battles amusing?" he asked no one in particular.

One of the bigger aliens on Rotciv's crew gave a war cry and charged, swinging a mace.

Five heads looked over the barrier, all of them watching him run toward them.

"Um," Tabitha looked around, "anyone?"

Katsu fired some sort of alien shotgun and the blast dropped him in his tracks, but his body nearly flipped from its force and he ended up skidding toward them, bloody and headless.

"Whoa." Tabitha peered out from behind the concrete but pulled her head back quickly when another soldier shot at her. "That was both cool and disgusting in equal parts."

"Go back to your ship and get out of this sector," Rotciv yelled. "Last warning!"

"All right, Tontos." Tabitha's eyes began to glow, and her teeth lengthened. "Let's go show this asshole what's what. Pull your swords. I bet none of these gutless bastards will even think of coming after us."

Hirotoshi unsheathed his sword "This does not count against your push-ups, Kemosabe."

"What kind of plan is that?" Ryu asked.

Tabitha stuck her tongue out at Hirotoshi. "I can always hope I die here and leave you to suck it that I failed to do the push-ups."

She stood up and charged out into battle, yelling. Her Tontos sprang up and followed her at top speed.

"I hope she's right!" Katsu yelled to Ryu, jumping over a small boulder.

"This is a *terrible* plan!" Ryu yelled back. He was laughing, though.

Tabitha was right. The sight of five vampires charging at them, four of whom had swords, had a marked effect on Rotciv's soldiers. Most of them broke and ran, screaming, and those who didn't at least stopped shooting.

Rotciv took off like a shot, and Tabitha sprinted to close the distance between them.

He dodged around trees and hacked his way through the forest, doubling back sometimes and trying to evade her, but at last Tabitha tackled him into a small clearing.

He struggled, scaly green arms pushing against her. "You are a nasty human!" He slapped her across the face.

She punched the shit out of him, and lights started dancing in front of him.

"Rotciv," she announced, "you're under arrest." She hauled him up and gave Hirotoshi, who had caught up, a look. "Doing it by the book. For Shin."

Hirotoshi nodded. *"For Shin."*

"C'mon, asshole." Tabitha started dragging Rotciv back

toward the main landing area. He was yelling about how he wouldn't go back to prison, and she just rolled her eyes.

"I assume you have a plan, Kemosabe?" Hirotoshi asked as they ducked under a limb.

"I do, Number One. And it's a really, *really* good one," Tabitha replied.

I'm not going to like this, he thought to himself.

"Let's go back to Farha Station," she declared.

Nope. He sighed as he rubbed his jaw. *I don't.*

"We're going back to Farha?" Ryu's voice came from ahead of them.

"Bet you didn't think I'd say that, did you?" She watched Katsu and Ryu head into the ship.

"Yeah, we're going back." Tabitha grinned. "The *rest* is a surprise."

Borven stomped down the hallway to his temporary office on Farha Station.

The past day and a half had been nothing but frustration.

First, that human had outwitted him, which had been embarrassing enough, but then they had managed to override the station controls and leave before he could take them into custody.

Now he couldn't even find out anything about their ship or last known port of call. All trails began and ended in the Etheric Empire, and they didn't share data with outsiders.

He'd been angling for a promotion, but as soon as he

put through the paperwork on this particular mission, he was going to have to kiss that hope goodbye.

He was still grumbling as he came around the door... and saw a human waiting for him in his office. She was perched cross-legged on his desk. When he came around the corner, she straightened up and gave him a cheery wave.

"Hi, Borven."

"Ranger Two." He had found out her identity while trying to figure out where to find her.

From what he had read of her, he *wanted* to like her. She was known not to have any patience for people trying to get out of paying their dues, and she'd done some pretty impressive things. She seemed to have a particular hatred for Skaines.

But she had also almost singlehandedly cost him his next promotion, so he couldn't quite *bring* himself to like her.

"I have something for you," she told him. If she was put off by his grumpy manner, she didn't let on. She uncurled her long legs from the desk and stood up, beckoning him over to look at the security feeds.

Borven scanned through them. He didn't see anything unusual, and finally he shrugged and looked at her.

"What?"

"There." She pointed to one of the cells in the station's tiny brig. "*That* is Rotciv."

"You *found* him?" Borven dropped into his seat, landing with a grunt. His face broke into a smile. "This is the best news I've had in..." He thought for a moment. "Weeks, honestly. I knew he was up to something, and with him locked up now …" He looked at her. "Well, I'll admit, that *is* a nice present."

"Oh, it's not just that he's locked up." Tabitha was bouncing on the soles of her feet. "You'll *also* find documentation that *you* found out where he was and sent me after him." She pointed to his computer. "I put it all in, backdated. No one will find out. Unless they're a better hacker than me, of course… But," She tilted her head to the side, considering, "*that's* unlikely."

For a moment, Borven didn't understand. Then he frowned at her.

"What… Why would you… Why are you doing this for *me*?" With the records changed *this* mission would be an incredible success for him, and the promotion was a solid possibility once more.

She looked at him. "I wanted to say I was sorry." Tabitha shrugged. "I know I annoyed you, running off like that. Truth is, I've been…" She cleared her throat and looked away. "It's not important. Anyway, I know you've been looking for Rotciv," she pointed, "and here he is."

He eyed her. "Thank you. Will you, uh…" He scratched his head. "Can I do anything for you?"

"Don't think so." She was already most of the way out the door, and she waved over her shoulder. "Byeeeee!"

Borven stared after her and began to laugh. He shook his head and turned around in his chair to grab a piece of fruit, still chuckling.

Ranger Two. What a character. He'd never met anyone quite like *her* before.

Rebus Quadrant, Aboard the *Penitent Granddaughter*

The flight had been calm, enough so that it was a bit hard to believe there had been a full-scale battle and execution just a few hours beforehand. Somehow, the fact that Grim and Nickie were enjoying a steak on the bridge seemed surreal in contrast to the earlier situation.

"No Durq?" Nickie asked, talking around a full mouth as she shoveled in the last few bites of steak. "Or is he still hiding under his bed?"

"He's eating in his room," Grim replied, his plate already empty. "I'm sure he'll join us if he feels like it."

Nickie grunted in acknowledgment and Grim reached for the wine bottle. They were quiet as he refilled their glasses, until finally, he hedged carefully, "Quite a show you put on earlier with the captain."

Nickie snorted and lifted her glass to take a long gulp. "I thought it was pretty well done, yeah," she agreed. "Besides, the fucker deserved it."

"No one said he didn't," Grim assured her and took a sip of wine. "It just seemed a touch...*over-done*. I mean, a public execution? Really? In front of a bunch of already-traumatized colonists?"

Nickie scowled across the table at him and busied herself taking another long gulp of her wine. "None of them seemed to mind all that fucking much at the time," she pointed out waspishly, folding her arms on the table and hunching over them. "They seemed right as rain."

"That's not how PTSD works," Grim reminded her blandly.

Though she looked irritated, she conceded after a moment, "Maybe it *was* a bit much, but you can't deny it had a dramatic effect."

Grim hummed in agreement, but it took a few seconds for him to respond verbally. He idly twirled the contents of his glass as he thought. "I suppose. But...I don't know. You just seem angry about something."

The bridge lapsed into tense silence after that, as Nickie scowled down at the table and left Grim to simply wait for something to happen. Several minutes passed before she gulped the rest of her wine and set the glass down with more force than was strictly necessary.

"I had an aunt," she finally stated. "Well, *have*, I guess. She's still out there. Big fucking deal with the Skaines. She was like their monster under the bed. And—God, I fucking adored her," she grumbled, her hands tightening into fists against the table. "And you know what she does? She goes haring off into the galaxy with barely a backward glance like I'm just an afterthought. I never really know where she is, and I wouldn't be surprised if I never actually saw her again."

She glared at her glass as if the fact that it was empty had somehow personally offended her.

Grim took a moment to finish his wine, steadying his nerves. "I know what that's like, losing people you figured would always be there. It's like part of the universe has been swallowed."

Nickie nodded along with what he said, her expression thoughtful. When she didn't reply immediately, Grim asked slowly, "Have you heard about Borderline Personality Disorder?"

She glared at him half-heartedly as she replied, "You aren't a shrink, Dr. Armchair."

"I'm not," he agreed readily, shrugging briefly. "But I wanted to be for a while before the rest of the universe decided not to cooperate."

He paused after that, watching her expectantly. It didn't take long before she heaved a sigh and said, "Fiiiiiine. Shoot. Tell me about this borderline whatever-it-is."

"Borderline Personality Disorder is... Well, it can be a lot of things, but the crux is, it means someone is pathologically afraid of being abandoned," he explained, running a finger around the edge of his wine glass just for something to do with his hands. "They either cling way too much to people they have, or they push them away to get it over with and have some control over it. Or they just refuse to reach out at all, so then no one gets a chance to leave." He glanced up at her as he finished, "It can be pretty self-fulfilling, but it doesn't actually have to be."

Nickie's eyes narrowed slightly. "What are you getting at?"

Grim sighed with exaggerated patience. "I'm saying that I'm not going anywhere. I'm not going to just up and leave you."

There was silence in the room for a moment. Nickie frowned as she turned that thought over in her head as if trying to examine it from every angle. She jumped slightly when Grim leaned across the table to point a finger at her nose.

"Which means," he continued, "that you can stop being *such a monumental jackass.*"

Nickie whooped out a startled bark of laughter, one hand flying up to clap over her mouth as Grim leaned away again, looking very satisfied with himself. She sniggered a few more times before she got herself under control enough to assure him, "I, uh… I'll be sure to take that under advisement from now on!"

When she calmed down, she leaned away from the table, stretching toward the captain's chair. There was a tiny cupboard under it. It wasn't standard with the make and model of the ship, so she had to assume the captain had installed it. And good thing, too. Nickie popped the latch and pulled out a bottle of brandy.

"Can I tempt you?" she asked, trying for coy and landing more in the ballpark of mischievous. If Grim minded, he didn't show any indication.

Instead, all he said was, "Don't mind if I do."

The wine glasses weren't clean, so they were perfectly content to just pass the bottle back and forth.

Rebus Quadrant, Aboard the *Penitent Granddaughter,* Nickie's Quarters

Nickie lay on her bed, boots off now and wearing a night suit, reading the last part of the entry in her aunt's diary.

Grim had long since retired to his quarters, but his words about her personality traits echoed in her mind even as she read about her aunt's adventures.

As Nickie pondered, her consciousness drifting, she wondered again why her aunt would set up her entries to only reveal themselves now.

Maybe she knew something about what Nickie would be facing? How she would be feeling?

But then, what was she hoping Nickie would take from this story? That killing Skaines in anger isn't good for her? It was pretty much what Grim had told her, albeit in a roundabout way.

And what of this Angie? Was she comparing her pain— the pain of losing her favorite aunt—with the pain Angie was going through?

It seemed a strange way to cast a story within a story. It must mean something.

But Nickie wasn't struggling with a broken heart.

Or maybe that was the point.

Maybe she was.

And maybe she was using the theatrics and the rambunctiousness to...

"No!" she called, then clamped a hand over her mouth.

Shit.

She listened, hoping no one else had heard her. It would

be major-league embarrassing to explain to Grim that she was talking to herself.

Okay, so maybe she did have feelings about her aunt still. Maybe it was heartbreak. But that could wait for another day.

She needed to get some rest.

Mere, lights out, please.

As you wish.

The lights in her quarters dimmed to blackness, leaving her to roll over under the covers and drift off into a well-deserved sleep.

CHAPTER 21 TABITHA

Farha Station, Aboard the *Achronyx*

In the main living area of the *Achronyx*, Tabitha gave a happy sigh and propped her feet up on the couch. It had been two days since she'd delivered Rotciv and his lieutenants to Borven, and since then the *Achronyx* had been docked at the station.

At Borven's pained request, she hadn't gotten into any *really* good bar fights. But even he had admitted that station rules were station rules, and if individual bartenders didn't mind the fights as long as she paid the tab, he wouldn't intervene.

So they'd been able to have some fun. She and Okk had even managed to come to an understanding—they both loved fights, and they both loved spitting crazy insults at people, so as soon as they saw each other in a bar, they'd start pounding on each other without any delay.

She'd come to think of Okk as a good friend. Hirotoshi

said she was crazy, and Tabitha privately thought that he was just mad that Okk kept insulting his looks.

Hirotoshi didn't like to let on, because he considered it a personal failing of his, but he was really very vain.

Other than the bar fights, however, it had been a very slow couple of days. Don Guido had passed on a few tidbits of information that would lead to some good jobs —even a piece of information on a Skaine ship carrying stolen grain—but Tabitha was in no hurry. The grain would still be in the hold of that ship for a few more days.

She could relax a little bit.

She scrambled to sit properly when Hirotoshi came into the room. He tended to get on her case for putting her feet on the furniture. He only gave her an amused glance, however, and went to make himself some tea.

She waited, curious. Hirotoshi hadn't spoken to her privately since they had come back to Farha Station, and she still wasn't sure what he had thought of her choice to turn Rotciv over to a government other than the Etheric Empire.

When he came out of the small kitchen to take a seat he was smiling, however.

"So…" he began.

"So?" Tabitha crossed her legs and bounced slightly in her seat. "What about that gun, huh? Can take down *trees*."

"Perhaps not its most efficient use," Hirotoshi replied diplomatically. "What I mean is, you don't seem as disappointed as I expected."

"What do I have to be disappointed about?" Tabitha asked. She settled back in her seat, frowning in confusion.

"Rotciv wasn't Skaine," Hirotoshi pointed out. "Your whole Skaine eradication plan…"

"Oh." Tabitha looked grumpy. "You want me to do all those push-ups. It's going to take so long," she complained. "*So* long."

"You lost that bet fair and square." Hirotoshi took a sip of his tea. "But I wasn't referring to the push-ups. I meant that you haven't mentioned the Skaines since that operation. We figured we'd be following some more Skaine trails."

"Oh." Tabitha shrugged. "I mean, I guess." She put her knees up and wrapped her arms around them. She chewed on her lip. "I think I needed to work some stuff out about Shin's death. I stopped thinking about *why* a Ranger exists. Borven reminded me. Rotciv reminded me. Don't think I'll go *easy* on any Skaines we find," she added.

Hirotoshi laughed. "I wouldn't dream of being that stupid, Kemosabe." He smiled at her. "It's good to have you back." He stood and went off to do…whatever it was that he did when he was alone. She had always pictured him doing a lot of paperwork, but she realized now that there wasn't much paperwork to do.

Maybe he read. She'd have to convince Achronyx to spy on him and tell her what he did. Then she could get him a book for Christmas.

Tabitha smiled after him as he left and propped her chin on her knees.

She still missed Shin terribly. She regretted his death. The pain hadn't gotten any less since they had come to this sector. In fact, she could almost say his loss hurt more than it had before.

But she wasn't covering the hurt with anger anymore. She wasn't on a blind quest for revenge.

She was beginning to heal at last.

Yoll Quadrant, QBSS *Meredith Reynolds*, Never Submit-Never Surrender Bar

"And that was how it happened," Tabitha finished. She drained her beer and smiled at Angie. "In the end, what it took was…"

Her voice trailed off, and she waited for Angie to finish the sentence. She wondered what the gunnery officer had taken from this story. Angie struck her as a tangle of contradictions: fiercely competent but very unsure of herself, funny but shy, a dreamer unwilling to see that she was living her dreams.

"You had to learn that no one could grieve *for* you," Angie replied. She looked at Tabitha. "If you had taken their advice at the start, you wouldn't have grieved. Grief is something you can't skip."

Tabitha nodded. "That is a good way of saying it." Lilah had set a new beer beside her, and she lifted it to clink it against Angie's glass. "To Manny."

Angie didn't hesitate. "To Shin."

The two women drank, and each pretended not to see the glitter of tears in the other's eyes. *People die in war,* Lilah had said, and it was true. You became accustomed to it in a strange way, but Angie realized now that you never got *over* it.

She wondered if she had been putting off her grieving because she was afraid to stop loving Manny, and decided she had. The idea of moving on with her life had seemed like a terrible betrayal of him.

But she saw now that she was never going to forget him, and that her grief was killing her while she tried to keep it from running its course.

Beside her, Tabitha considered as she drank, and now she said, "Sometimes it's about who you share the story with that helps you get past the painful parts." She nodded at Terrence. "Terrence here has listened to this story… what, twenty times?"

Terrence laughed easily. "Thirty at least. And it gets better every time we hear it."

"You appreciate it more each time?" Angie guessed.

He gave a wicked grin. "Well, that, and…let's just say Ranger Two adds a bit of 'flavor' every time she tells it."

"She never contradicts herself, either," George added. "Over the years, we've come to wonder if she's just telling different *parts* of the same story."

"Or if she's making stuff up," Terrence added.

Everyone laughed, including Tabitha. She gave Angie a conspiratorial wink. "A lady never tells."

Angie laughed and watched the regulars. She wondered what had brought each of them here to listen to Tabitha's story. What loss had Terrence faced? What about George? She saw an older woman with streaks of gray just beginning to show in her blonde hair. The woman nodded at Angie and smiled.

She had been inducted into a small club, she realized.

"We'd love to hear about Manny," Terrence suggested, "if you wanted to tell us."

Angie felt the instinctive desire to close everything off and stop speaking, but she forced her way through it and nodded. She held up one finger as she fought for composure.

Finally, she said, "He was a Guardian Marine."

Everyone nodded appreciatively, and a smile broke over her face. "He loved it. It was everything to him, even the parts other people thought were a drag. Waking up at five for PT, for instance."

Everyone laughed, and a few people nodded knowingly.

"He saw almost everything like that as an opportunity to get better," Angie explained. "And the rest, well, he just told himself he'd get through it so he could go back to doing the stuff he really liked."

She was stalling for time, but it took a lot of courage to speak about his death.

Finally, she found it. "Both our ships were in the battle that killed him. We were in orbit above Faden. It's a small planet, not really important, but that's where we met with the Leath. Our ship was up in orbit, and his team was on the surface. I was afraid for him. I was always afraid when he was getting shot at, right?"

They nodded.

"It was a one-in-a-million chance, though," Angie continued. She sighed and clenched her hands. "The Leath captain, he was… God, he was a stupid jackass. He tried to skip his ship off the planet's atmosphere to get away, and one of our ships saw what he was doing and went to shoot him down. And they did." She looked down at the table, not really seeing it at all. "The pieces of the ship were big enough that some of them made it to the ground. Manny was one of the ones hit."

There was silence when she finished talking.

"Was it your ship?" Terrence asked curiously. "That shot him down, I mean."

"No, thank God." Angie shook her head. "I know no one could have predicted that, but to believe that I might have ordered the shot and then... That would have just killed me." She shook her head at her choice of words. "God, what am I even saying?"

"We get it," Terrence assured her.

She met his brown eyes and saw that he really did. Whatever loss Terrence had experienced, he understood the phases of it.

Angie looked at Tabitha. "It did help to tell it. It really did. Thank you."

Tabitha smiled. As Angie looked away, lost in thought, Tabitha's eyes strayed to the glass. Angie had clearly come in here hoping to get blind drunk, but now that she'd gotten the grief off her chest, she was no longer drinking. Tabitha didn't think Angie had touched her beer since the break in the story.

Tabitha smiled at Terrence, and the two of them nodded at one another.

Another soul was starting to heal.

FINIS

AUTHOR NOTES - ELL LEIGH CLARKE

WRITTEN JULY 21, 2018

Thank Yous

Massive thanks as always goes out to MA, my collaborator on this project. This is another one of those books like in the Second Dark Ages series where we each wrote half the words, and then one of us (yours truly) has the task of stitching it all together.

Can you guess who did what? ;)

Thanks MA for letting me in on another Kurtherian project. It's been a blast.

Huge thank yous also go to Steve "Zen Master" Campbell and the JIT team who work tirelessly to make sure that all slips are caught and corrected, the files are uploaded on time.

Thank you so much folks. I truly appreciate all your efforts. :)

Reviewers

Massive thanks also goes out to our dedicated and

engaged Amazon reviewers. It's because of you that we get to do this full time. Without your five-star reviews and thoughtful words on the Zon we simply wouldn't have enough folks reading these space shenanigans to be able to write full time.

You are the reason these stories exist and you have no idea how frikkin' grateful I am to you.

Truly, thank you.

Readers and FB page supporters

Last, and certainly by no means least, I'd like to thank you for reading this book, and giving a new series a try. I'm hoping you've enjoyed it!

Your enthusiasm for the world, and the characters, is heart-warming. Your words of encouragement, and demands for the next episode, are the things that often stay in my mind as I flick from checking the facebook page to the scrivener file when I start each writing session.

Thank you for being here, for reading, for reviewing, and for always brightening my day with your words of support on the fb page. You rock my world, and without you, there really would be no reason to write these stories.

Thank you.

E x

Jayne Austin and Impossible Deadlines

If you followed the (now complete!) Molly series you have probably seen us talk about the Jayne Austin, Spy for Hire series in a bit of detail in our author notes.

You may also have seen me mention that were planning on doing a rapid release on this new series: three books in the space of a month. It takes about a month to write each one though, so we delay the door launch date of the first one until the third one is the ready: effectively "saving them up".

Unfortunately, even though MA knows this, having been the guy that told me about it, when he hears me say when we plan to launch the first one he has this as:

Oh, I don't have to do anything on this until the last two weeks. That's good!

No. No MA. You do not get to do that! Someone has to find time to write all these things before we hit publish!

(I have eyerolls on tap.)

X-ray Vision and Poker

MA and I were talking about the Jayne, Spy for Hire series that we've been working on for a few months now.

MA suggested that in order to win at poker Jayne should use some kind of x-ray vision gadget/implants, in order to see her opponent's cards. <Michael – I don't remember this! Not saying I didn't say it...just don't remember saying it ;-) >

Ellie: You know that would be cheating right?

MA: Yeah, she's a dubious character...

Ellie: I guess she is now.

Giggles all round.

MA and Bragging

Sometimes it's hard working with a collaborator who has multiple other projects going on at any one time. Even with the best will in the world some things fall through the cracks. For a while I was trying to get him to do some work on these beats for the Tabatha side of the story. Imagine my joy when I wake up one morning and is posted on Facebook that he's been working on his beats, and that is working with Ell Leigh Clarke later today!

Woot!

Traction. Finally. Something is happening...

Optimistic, I showed up to our story meeting later that afternoon.

Ellie (beaming): so I see that you've been working on your beats?

MA: oh yeah I posted the earlier, about this meeting.

Ellie: (teasing) yeah I noticed how you were bragging that you were putting the work in. Let's see them then?

Ellie waits expectantly.

MA turns bright red.

Ellie: What? What is it? We were meant to be working on these today right?

MA: Er...

Ellie (slow realization): you haven't got the beats?

MA: not really.

Ellie: But you were bragging to the fans?

MA: Yeah. I got sidetracked.

<Michael: WOW.... I just got busted...AGAIN!>

MA and Largesse

You may have seen the pre-order email for this book: beyond the frontier in the days leading up to the release. I noticed it come through one afternoon and took a peek to see how Tabitha would describe the release.

I must say I was impressed. The email was fun, witty and just the right amount of snark.

In fact, I was so impressed that I forwarded it to MA expressing that this was the best Tabitha email that I've ever seen.

His response?

Hahahahaha....

In general the feedback on the cover has been positive - so I have to give it to you on this cover...

Just not yet - the author notes aren't done ;-)
    Michael Anderle

(He'd been reticent about the cover design and he and Jeff had given me shit over my mockup when I presented the idea.)

Ellie response:
    This is so going in my author notes!

MA response:
    ... fuck ...

you'd take advantage of my largesse so easily?

I'm not sure, but I don't think it's largesse if it's not given freely and unreservedly...

And regarding the cover design, I have video footage of him and Jeff giving me shit over the concept it's based on. Keep your eyes on the fb/ lawnfaries youtube page for the footage. Brittany will be getting it posted soon.

    <Michael: Oh yeah, I gave her an asteroid full of shit on this

one... A few of you could help me out and voice a slight disagree-
ment... But only if you really feel it, because...because...
<SIGH>>

Space Odyssey: 2001

You may have seen on Facebook that I recently went to the cinema with my writer friend, Amy. We booked in several weeks ago to see the restoration version of Space Odyssey.

(We've been trying to do a film each week. It's a fun way to get away from the keyboard and do something fun but also good for our storytelling brains!)

I didn't quite know what to expect from Space Odyssey, but the Alamo cinemas have excellent boozy milkshakes and quite honestly as long as something isn't gory or scary I can watch almost anything. Even the artsy stuff.

The Alamo also has this great philosophy around film. Rather than just showing trailers, for about half an hour before the main feature it will show mini programs, documentaries, clips and generally just cultural stuff to do with the show you're about to see. (I took some pictures of one of the cartoons about gravity and posted them with a selfie on Facebook.)

A number of folks asked me what I thought of the movie. I have lots of thoughts to share, but were limited on word count here at the back of the book now, so I'll probably end up sharing them elsewhere in more detail, but here are a couple of takeaways.

What occurred to me as I watched the long, (often deafeningly loud) scenes were the influence this probably had on Interstellar. (I noticed a few of the people mentioned this in the comments and I totally agree.)

The other was about the hilarious scene where HAL explained that the whole crew are dead. I'm pretty sure that the creators of Red Dwarf were paying homage to this in their opening scene of the TV show.

If you haven't seen it, do check it out here: https://youtu.be/nyKF2qd0-iQ?t=2m43s

It's a British classic that my cool babysitter got me into when I was a kid. If you like British humour, you'll love it.

If you like the Scouse (Liverpool) accent, you'll be mesmerized.

Coffee and Space Travel

<Michael: Was there something that was going to be right here?>

<< Ellie: Oops. Yeah. Ok, so here's the story…

On the way to see Space Odyssey we passed by a Starbucks. We were heading down town and I don't normally venture that far, so it's become unusual for me to see a big ass Starbucks.

I comment on it, with a sigh leaving Amy to explain to the Lyft driver that I'm off ALLLL caffeine, on doctor's orders.

The Lyft driver expresses his sympathy, and the conversation moves on.

Until we get into the cinema… where I notice a guy a couple of seats down from us has ordered a big ass caffetiere of coffee. Amy catches me gawking, then sniffs at the air. "Hmm, that coffee smells good!" she teased.

I sulked for a full twenty seconds.

Eventually the movie began and some time after that, the story got going. (If you've seen the film you'll know what I'm talking about!). Not many scenes into the actual story there are three guys heading out to the moon to investigate a secret phenomenon.

We watch as one of them unpacks turkey sandwiches and passes them around and the three chinwag about the operation as casually as if there were having a meeting in a board room. Mid way through their conversation the sandwiches guy offers them coffee... then turns around with a big ass space canister of caffeinated goodness.

Amy whacks me with her arm so hard I nearly snort my rum infused milkshake!

We sniggered, starting others around us to also snigger.

(I'm pretty sure they didn't know what was so funny... but I guess that is the beauty of a shared cinematic experience!)

I told her in the interval: "Even the guys in space get to drink coffee. How is that fair?" >>

Fours are soooo dramatic!

A couple of my friends here in Austin are into the Enneagram. They use it to make sense of a lot of the crazy people around us: their motivations, their reactions to things, the way they express themselves. If you've read any of my non-fiction you'll know that I already find profiling can be a useful tool for all of the above, and lots more.

Well, recently when we were doing one of our writing dates in the local café, (where Sven our curious barista takes care of us and waxes on about how fascinating we are

– even when we talk about ridiculous things like library books and other mundanities).

Amy mentioned that someone she knows is such a four. I asked what that meant, and she explained that fours are dramatic, and artists, and sometimes special snowflakes.

Oh, I said. *What is my number?*

She and Alyssa exchanged glances.

Alyssa had previous had me pegged as a nine, but now she reconsidered. After answering a few questions she had me read a short passage she had on her phone.

Omg – that is totally me! I exclaimed, surprised to finally be reading something that made sense. (In the past I've been profiles and tested and not really bought into the description 100%).

Alyssa: You're a four.

Ellie: you mean, the overly dramatic one?

Amy: Yes. Exactly that.

<Michael: BWAHAHAHAHAHAHAHAHAHA ...<inhale deeply and for a while> HAHAHAHAHAHAHA!>

Now, ever since, whenever Amy describes me as "being SOoooo dramatic" I have a ready-made excuse.

That's just coz I'm a four, I tell her.

She looks at me dryly, perhaps wishing she'd never giving me such a neatly packaged come-back.

And so it goes on.

Well, for the last few weeks my acupuncturist has been checking a point on my inner thigh for a needle bruise... ever since I said I've had a permanent tattoo there ever since I started acupuncture. (Ok, maybe it was a slight exaggeration, but he's made a thing to check it every time now... just to prove me wrong.)

So once again, for maybe the 14th time, he checks it. "Nope, no bruise," before he proceeds to jab a needle into the spot in question.

"It's ok if there ever is a bruise there. It's not a big deal," I say, trying to normalize the situation. "I'm not going to die from a tiny bruise."

"Oh my god, you're so dramatic!" he replied.

Even though I said I'm NOT going to die!

Somehow I'm still the one that's dramatic.

I then *had* to explain the enneagram to him, and that my friends think I'm a four.

He agreed with Alyssa's diagnosis as he ambled out having covered my body with hellraiser pins.

<Michael: This is SUCH a good description!>

E x

P.S. I've just launched a Patreon account. If you'd like to see more pictures, happenings and read more author notes, feel free to check it out over here: https://www.patreon.com/ellleighclarke

AUTHOR NOTES - MICHAEL ANDERLE

WRITTEN JULY 1`, 2018

First, I thank you for not only reading this book, but also working your way through the author notes to what we have to say here.

Since my collaborator in crime, Ellie, has taken up so much of the last part of this book with her notes I believe that I have to cut mine very short. Therefore, it is with much sadness that I have to say I'm done.

Ad Aeternitatem,

Michael Anderle

.

.

.

BWAHAHAHAHAHA! <I am imagining Ellie as she first believes that I stopped with only writing a short Author

269

Note (and shirking my job), then quickly realizing that I continued on.

<NOW she is realizing (with narrowed eyebrows) that I am harassing her from afar.>

<< Ellie edit: and also seeing that your author notes are only 800 words even though you carry on. You had waaaay more words you could have written. Don't be blaming me for a word limit. You're nowhere near it! >>

Serves you right for placing in the author notes related to the front cover! I should have known that you would not provide me the littlest amount of reprieve. Mind you, with the sheer amount of harassment I gave you during the creation of the cover, I suppose it might be warranted.

(For those who wish to understand just how much fun Jeff and I had, connect with Ell Leigh Clarke's Facebook page and you will get notified. Or I suppose she might mention it in the emails.)

<< Ellie edit: I will. >>

Expensive Taste

So, I am minding my own business on Facebook the other day when I get notified that Ellie has placed a new Facebook post up. Often, her posts can be fun, and occasionally interesting too. (Yes, I'm getting the narrowed eyebrows again.)

<< Ellie edit: now I'm getting paranoid about my eyebrows. Since when do brows narrow?? >>

This time, my eyes shrink themselves as I realize she has a picture of a whiskey bottle on her Facebook page.

Now, I realize that she drinks upon occasion, but

placing a whiskey bottle up on Facebook, at least to my knowledge, isn't something that she normally does. So, being the inquisitive inspector Clouseau that I am, I look further into this.

Originally, I did not remember what was on the whiskey bottle, so I had to leave these notes and go find out.

The bottle says, "LAPHROIAIG" 10 year Single Malt Whisky.

Now, inside my mind I'm thinking, "I can't even pronounce the name, how is one supposed to drink something you can't pronounce?" (I'm not a drinker much, I rely on my collaborators to add that verisimilitude.)

<< Ellie edit: by this you're inferring that you can pronounce all the chemicals in a bottle of coke? >>

BUT, it is her quote that goes with it that makes me chuckle. She says, "Damn my folks for instilling me with expensive taste in booze!"

I chuckle because the word 'booze' makes me laugh. (I don't know why, it seems like a dirty word and my 12 year old boy inside snickers.)

<< Ellie edit: I think there is a conflation with the word BOOBS going on in the mind of your inner 12 y.o! >>

Then, I "like" the post... and over the next few days I notice something. This post is going viral-ish. I just checked and it IS doing much better than her normal posts. It's like alcohol (and arguing about which kinds of whisky is the best) is a more contentious and enjoyable past-time than I would have thought.

It's like older, but yet still strikingly handsome, authors can learn something new every day.

<< Ellie edit: This reminds me of the meme...

"When 3 people have sex, it's called a threesome.

When 2 people have sex, it's called a twosome.

Now I understand why some people call themselves handsome." >>

"Jayne is Coming..."

We think.

Right now, we are in production on the Jayne Austin series. I think I have mentioned before, that the name of the protagonist is very on purpose.

Why? Well, first my collaborator is English. That seemed very apropos (Jane Austen is English as well, if you didn't know.)

Second, she was moving from Los Angeles to Austin, Texas and therefore the last name seemed pretty important.

Third, we added a "y" to the first name and changed the spelling from Austen to Austin, so that those that love the original Jane Austen series, won't come by and give us a bunch of one star reviews.

At least, that's my story and I'm sticking to it until Ellie provides me with a different one. Then, if it is a BETTER story, I might switch.

<< Ellie Edit: Nope. That's my story too. Until we come up with a better one! >>

Huh, I wonder which way Ellie spells "Austin."

Ok, this is going to be the actual end. I have been informed that she's added a few more words to her author notes, which probably puts her around the 2000 word mark.

These author notes will end up being about 800 words or so, which means that we will be getting just a little bit shy of 3000 words.

Our next Tabitha book will be coming out in August, look for it as you wind up your wonderful summer and get ready for a hopefully enjoyable fall.

<Ok, "Dragon Dictate" didn't record my ending correctly. So, I'm going to type the correct ending, and then share with you right after the correct one, what Dragon thought I said.>

Ad Aeternitatem,

Michael Anderle

Not this:
> *Add Attorney Tatum,*
> *Michelangelo*

Nor this:
> *Add to turn it to him,*
> *Michael handily*

And hell no:
> *Add the Turner Tatum,*
> *Michael and early*

<< Ellie Edit: Hahahahahahaha! P.S. With my additional comments you're now at 984 words!>>

BOOKS WRITTEN BY ELL LEIGH CLARKE

BOOKS WRITTEN BY MICHAEL ANDERLE

For a complete list of books by Michael Anderle, please visit

www.lmbpn.com/ma-books/

All LMBPN Audiobooks are Available at Audible.com and iTunes

CLICK HERE TO SEE ALL LMBPN BOOKS ON AUDIBLE

CONNECT WITH THE AUTHORS

Ell Leigh Clarke Social Links

Join Ellie's Email List here
http://ellleighclarke.com/

Facebook
http://www.facebook.com/ellleighclarke/

Website
http://ellleighclarke.com/

Michael Anderle Social Links

Join the email list here:

http://kurtherianbooks.com/email-list/

Join the Facebook Group Here:

**https://www.facebook.com/TheKurtherianGambitBoo
ks/**